Copyright © 2024 by Ellen ES Ceely

All rights reserved.

No part of this publication may be reproduced, distributed, or transmitted in any form or by any means, including photocopying, recording, or other electronic or mechanical methods, without the prior written permission of the publisher, except as permitted by U.S. copyright law. For permission requests, contact Ellen ES Ceely at ellen.es.ceely@gmail.com.

NO AI TRAINING: Without in any way limiting the author's [and publisher's] exclusive rights under copyright, any use of this publication to "train" generative artificial intelligence (AI) technologies to generate text is expressly prohibited. The author reserves all rights to license uses of this work for generative AI training and development of machine learning language models.

The story, all names, characters, and incidents portrayed in this production are fictitious. No identification with actual persons (living or deceased), places, buildings, and products is intended or should be inferred.

Book Cover by Ellen ES Ceely

Chapter Art by Corrie Bergmann

First edition 2024

eBook ISBN 978-1-962016-04-9
Paperback ISBN 978-1-962016-05-6

10 9 8 7 6 5 4 3 2 1

for Aleya and Lavinia

I am so proud of you
may you always find the courage to do what's right
may you always find a reason to live in the light
even when others fail
even when all seems lost
may you always find hope when darkness covers your sight.

Glass Mountain

The Marshlands

Star Forest

Sarilda's Castle

Kingdom of Eryas

One

The day I cut off my finger was the day I understood pain.

That pain destroyed my remaining innocence and naivete, but it became the architect of the deepest joy I've ever experienced. The determination with which I did it showed me who I am.

My name is Sarilda, princess of the Kingdom of Eryas, only daughter to King Otto and Queen Ada.

The day before my sixteenth birthday began as most any other day. Waking at dawn, I washed my face, pulled my training stays over my tunic and riding pants, and grabbed my bow, throwing knives, and sword.

My father's greatest pride and deepest regret was teaching me to fight, throw knives, and shoot as well as his best guards. But as his only child and heir to the throne, what choice did he have?

Circling the captain in front of me, the thought of my birthday was at the forefront of my mind as emotions swirled inside my head.

"Princess Sarilda," Captain Bastian called to me, delivering a swift knock to my behind with the flat of his blade. "Focus!"

With a grimace, I twirled back around, annoyed that I'd been so easily distracted. *That's going to leave a bruise.* I thought. *At least tomorrow will be spent dancing and not sitting. However, I must repay the favor before my training session is done.*

Clenching my sword in my right hand, I held a throwing knife in my left.

Brown hair fell out of the tight braid I'd twisted into a bun as I'd gotten ready for the day. Curls swinging into my line of sight, I puffed air out of my pursed lips to chase the rogue tendrils away.

Focus. I told myself, locking my eyes on Captain Bastian. *If he wants me to focus, then I'll show him the meaning of the word.*

I turned in a tight circle with the captain, our swords meeting. Our knives engaged, and then pushed away from each other like a couple caught in a deadly dance.

Off to one side, I heard a whisper from a soldier, but caught nothing other than the captain's name. So did he. In an instant, I was behind him, using his distraction to my advantage.

The crisp fall morning had given way to a hot fall day, the sun unrelenting overhead. The white stones of the shore beneath our feet reflected the heat back into our faces. The cool saltwater lapped along the shore a few feet away.

I landed a quick *smack* to his backside, before twirling again and placing my knife at the base of his collarbone.

"Do you yield, Captain?" I asked, my breath shallow as sweat dripped down my back.

Captain Bastian grinned at me. "I do, indeed, yield." He said. "And I acknowledge the hit. Well played, princess."

I returned his grin and backed away. Though I was tall and thin, he still towered over me, my head barely reaching his chin. To defeat him was always a feat I took pride in.

"I believe it's time you went back to the castle for lunch." He said, sheathing his sword and snapping his knife back on his belt. Following suit, I glanced up at the high noon sun. "Your mother gave me strict instructions that I was to leave plenty of time for a final dress fitting this afternoon."

He nodded toward the trail leading from our rocky training ground. "If there's time, come find me by the stables and we'll work on your shooting." He bowed, then turned back to his soldiers with a smirk.

Sighing, I turned and made my way toward the trail. As much as I loved the dress my mother had commissioned for my birthday, I longed to stay behind and eat bread and cheese and dried meat with the soldiers.

I'd rather dip my feet in the cold water while I eat than sit in the high-backed chair and drink hot tea with my mother. I thought.

The shade of the forest path was a welcome retreat from the heat of the shore. No matter how much I wanted to stay, to feel I was something more than the King's daughter, I had to admit the relief of the trees was welcome.

Winding my way over the path, I climbed up the hillside toward the castle that towered beside the gentle Mer Sea. Birds sang above me, following as I walked along. Red, yellow, and orange leaves crunched beneath my feet, infusing the air with their earthy scent.

Other than the peaceful chirping of birds and the crunching beneath my feet, the trees were silent and calm. None moved to change my course, they merely watched as I found my way through the woods.

The castle loomed overhead as I exited the woods. I squinted and shielded my eyes with a hand as the white stones of the castle glistened in the bright sun. The flower gardens basked in the bright rays, clinging to the last bit of warmth for the season.

Ahead, at the entrance of the gardens, a woman waited for me. My steps faltered slightly as I considered the upcoming afternoon, but I pushed on. My mother, Queen Ada, was tall and thin like me.

But where my skin was tanned brown by the sun, hers was soft and fair, sheltered under the umbrella she held in her hand. While my eyes glinted gold, hers shone bright blue. Her hair was nearly as bright as the castle stones, and straighter than any I'd ever seen.

"How was training today, Sarilda?" Mother's gentle voice drifted across the space between us with effortless grace. I could not remember a day in which she'd raised it above a stern command.

"Good, mother. Sorry I'm late." I said, picking up on the nervous energy flowing from her and assuming I must be tardy. "I came back as soon as Captain Bastian told me to."

She smiled, a hint of sadness breaking through. "Not at all, child. You're not late." She held out a hand to me as I drew near and I took it. "Actually, I wish you could've stayed a bit longer."

"Are you alright, mother?" I asked, tilting my head with concern as her voice cracked. "What's wrong?"

For a moment, we stared at one another. I waited for her to answer, feeling as though she were on the verge as her face contorted with a thousand and one emotions.

"Nothing." She said, smiling and squeezing my hand. "Nothing you need concern yourself with. Come, let's go eat lunch so we can finish up your dress fitting for tomorrow."

Before I could ask any more questions, she dropped my hand. Picking up her skirts, she walked at a brisk pace through the gardens in the direction of her rooms.

Without another word, I followed, convinced she'd been about to tell me something important. *I can't make her tell me anything.* I thought.

Two

"It is my great honor, ladies and gentlemen, to present to you on her sixteenth birthday, Princess Sarilda of the Kingdom of Eryas."

My father's voice echoed through the ballroom, escaping as the doors opened and I entered the crowded room. A hush had fallen over the gathered gentry.

I glided down the center of the room toward where my parents stood at the opposite end of the ballroom in front of the King's banquet table. The eyes of every nobleman, king, queen, prince, and princess followed me.

Breathe. I told myself. *Don't look at them, just keep your eyes on mother. Take one step at a time and don't look around.* I locked eyes with my mother and her face broke into a smile.

I knew I looked good. My satin, cream-colored dress had been perfectly designed.

The lace from my petticoat peaked out beneath the skirt. A necklace of pale pink pearls hung at my throat, and my hair had been gathered into an intricate mass of braids and curls.

Being as tall as I was, my mother didn't put up a fight when I refused to wear anything other than soft, flat shoes made to match my dress.

When I reached my parents, I dipped into a deep curtsy, ducking my head before rising to meet my father's outstretched hand. We walked to the middle of the ballroom, just as we'd rehearsed for weeks on end.

The silence in the room was broken with the swell of the stringed orchestra in the corner of the room.

Picking up my skirts, I placed my left hand on my father's shoulder and my right hand in his outstretched palm. We waltzed around the room, the silent gathering of royalty and nobility slowly joining in and breaking their silence with excited chatter.

"You did well, Sarilda." My father said, smiling and turning with the music. "Now you can relax, dance, and enjoy the feast prepared for you."

Smiling up at him, I noticed a hint of sadness just as I had from my mother.

"What's wrong, father?" I asked, making sure to keep my smile plastered on my face and my voice quiet. "Don't tell me nothing, mother had the same worried expression on her face yesterday and all of today. Something's wrong."

He didn't answer me at first. We turned again, swirling with the music, nodding at guests as they waltzed beside us.

"Now is not the time, Sarilda." He said, a tight smile splayed across his lips. "We'll speak of it later." Before I could argue, the song ended. I curtsied as he bowed, and everyone paused to clap. First for me, then for the orchestra.

As soon as they began to play again, a young prince approached me and held out his hand as an invitation to dance, ducking his head. Without a word, my father turned to leave and I found myself eye to eye with one stranger after another.

I'd known the significance of my sixteenth birthday all my life. In everyone's eyes, I was of marriageable age. Going into the party, I knew that I'd be expected to dance with everyone who asked me unless I had good reason to turn them down.

But I had not expected so many princes, kings, and noblemen in attendance. And I'd not understood what it would be like to dance with everyone who asked.

They came to me in all shapes, sizes, and moods. Some were charming, but dull. Others were handsome, but uptight with foul breath and wandering hands. Some were small and petrified, never saying a word to me and looking everywhere but at my face.

I had partners who danced well and others who danced on my feet and not the floor. One old king held my hands and talked to me without ceasing, but never actually moved. A young nobleman twirled me around until I thought I might vomit.

Finally, after more than twenty dances, my mother approached and excused me from the prince who'd approached before the song could begin.

"My apologies," She said, smiling at the young man holding out his hand toward me. The stench of his rotting teeth reached me from a few feet away. Combined with the way he looked down his nose at me, I wondered if I would be able to keep from vomiting.

"My daughter needs to eat something on her birthday. As you can see, she's been dancing for quite some time and needs a rest." The young man appeared peeved, but there was no arguing with the Queen of Eryas.

"Yes, of course." He said, dropping his hand. "I was about to suggest the same thing and lead her to an empty seat." He paused, as if waiting to see if my mother would hand me over to him to get some food rather than caring for me herself.

"That is very thoughtful of you." Mother said, her smile widening as she took my hand in hers and tucked it into the crook of her arm. "I hope you'll invite Princess Sarilda to dance again later this evening." She nodded toward the prince, as if to dismiss him.

Clearly at a loss for words, he bowed to my mother and turned to leave.

"Thank you, Mother," I said, letting out a sigh of relief as we walked toward the table. She squeezed my hand in response and motioned for me to sit down beside her chair. "No, please," I said, hesitating to sit down. "Let me go to the feast table for food," I begged her with my eyes.

She hesitated, glancing around for a second to see who might be watching or listening. "I need a few moments alone. I promise I'll be back soon." I said, squeezing her hand with both of mine.

"Oh, very well. It is your birthday, after all."

Without another word, I picked up my skirts and slid along the wall toward the massive table of food along one side of the ballroom. I rounded the table to the servant's side without mishap, grabbed a plate, and piled it with everything that caught my eye.

Glancing around to see if anyone was watching, I ducked out the side door. Sinking to the ground in the servant's corridor, I dug into the food.

The music inside the ballroom and the dull hum of voices eased slightly. Servants passed me with nothing more than a quick nod or gentle curtsy, and overall I ate my supper in peace.

As I finished my food I got to my feet and handed the empty plate off to a servant passing by.

Time to go back in. I thought, taking a deep breath. Before I could round the corner of the doorway, the sound of angry voices reached my ears.

"If you think I'm going to wait for that brat of a girl of yours to grow up, you're sadly mistaken."

Freezing in place, I racked my brain for the identity of the man speaking.

"How dare you!"

That's father's voice. I thought, my ears ringing as I realized which girl the man was referring to.

"Don't play games with me, Otto." He hissed, the sound of a knife being unsheathed accompanying the threat. "You owe me a great debt. Now, I can collect by force, or you can do the right thing and spare the lives of your wife and daughter."

I held my breath, frozen in place as I waited for my father's response.

"Edward," his voice was calm, but the anger and fear permeating it were unmistakable. "She just turned sixteen. I have no intention of double-crossing you and every intention of repaying my debt." He paused and I longed to see what they were doing but I didn't dare move. "You've waited this long, what's the harm in waiting a few more weeks?"

Silence ensued.

"Let the children meet. Have Henry dance with Sarilda. Allow them the chance to get to know each other before we force them into an alliance."

"Very well," Edward replied, his knife slowly being sheathed. "You have eight weeks. In eight weeks time, your daughter marries my son by choice, or I come to Eryas and slaughter the lot of you."

My father inhaled and let out a groan, as though he'd been punched in the stomach. My blood ran cold. I wanted to run around the corner and attack the man, but I remained hidden.

"Do we have an understanding, *King* Otto?" The derision in Edward's voice was clear.

"Yes." Father hissed.

For a few more moments I remained hidden, giving time for them to move away from the door and for me to collect my wits. The rest of the night passed by in a blur.

With each new dance partner, I wondered which was Prince Henry and what debt my father owed his father that could only be paid by handing me over like chattel.

Three

My sleep was fitful the night of my birthday, and I woke exhausted with dark circles under my eyes. *Don't think about the dreams.* I told myself. *Ignore them, they're not reality.* But my mind wouldn't stop replaying the scenes of my forced marriage to a complete stranger.

Every time I'd tried to run and escape from the blurred face of King Edward or his son Henry, my father and mother would appear behind me. Linking arms and weeping, they would push me toward the marriage altar.

Dressing in my training gear once more, my fingers fumbled with the laces of my tunic, my stays, and my boots. Strapping my sword around my hips, I unsheathed one of the throwing knives and stared at it.

What would it be like to use it? I thought. *Every day I train, but I've never actually used my skills to take a life. What would happen if I did?* I imagined the unseeable face of King Edward as he threatened my father.

Stop it. I told myself. *The first thing you must do is talk to them, ask if it's true and why. Then ask why they waited so long to tell you.* The thought made me angry. The weight of the idea that they would keep such a vital piece of information secret from me was soul-crushing.

I'd thought about marriage. Just like anyone my age would. But I had always considered marriage to be a choice, something I would get to do for myself far in the future.

I wish things could stay the way they were. I thought as I sheathed my knife. *Oh, how I wish I'd never overheard the conversation.*

Pulling my hair back into a tight ribbon, I set my jaw and went to search for my parents. I found them in the breakfast room, both staring at their plates.

Mother's face looked haggard, old tears staining her cheeks. Father looked angry, as though he wanted to snap the plate in front of him in half.

"Good morning," I said, closing the door behind me. Neither of them looked up. Neither returned the greeting.

I sat in the chair opposite my mother, trying to force her to meet my gaze. She continued to stare at her plate, her eyes glued to the food she wasn't eating.

"Sarilda," Father said, clearing his throat. "Now that you're sixteen, we have something to discuss with you."

I continued to stare at my mother, unable to turn away from the despair covering her face.

"Does it have something to do with the conversation I overheard between you and King Edward last night?" I asked, pausing a minute to let my words sink in. "Does it have something to do with the fact that you're trading me over, selling me like chattel to a man you owe some great debt?" Anger overtook my voice.

"Your ears weren't meant for that conversation," Father replied after a second of shocked silence. "What were you doing spying on me?" His accusation broke the spell my mother's face had on me and I turned toward him.

"Spying on you?" I asked, incredulous. "I was eating food in the servant's corridor. Catching a break from men who trampled on my feet and called it dancing. I was partaking in the feast meant to celebrate my sixteenth birthday." I tried to calm my tone as my voice rose in volume. "When were you going to tell me you'd sold me off to the highest bidder?" Bitterness consumed me as I stared him down.

"It's not like that, Sarilda." He said, banging his fist on the table. Mother jumped in her seat and peered up at him in shock.

"Otto, we should explain, there's no need to be angry with her." Mother reached out as if to cover his hand with her own. But my father yanked his fingers away from her as if he'd been bitten by a snake.

"No need to be angry?" He shouted at her. "There is every reason to be angry." His gaze flicked back to mine. "I have given you everything you could ever want or need in life." He gestured to the room around us, tastefully decorated with tapestries. The eastern-facing floor to ceiling windows allowed early sunlight to stream into the room, and a fireplace glowed on the other side of the room with a warm fire.

"I've spoiled you, taught you to ride and fight like a man." His voice choked. "Like I would a son." He spoke the words through gritted teeth. "It's time you learned your place in this world, time you had the blanket of protection removed from around you so you can face reality."

He pushed away from the table and stomped to the nearest window, leaning against it as he surveyed the garden below.

"When you were a small child, your mother got very sick." His tone softened. "I searched far and wide for herbs, fairies, and all manner of healers to help her. Everyone I found told me the same thing: there was nothing they could do." He paused, as if considering his next words carefully.

"King Edward came to me with his palace healer. He said he could help, he could fix what ailed your mother."

Shifting in my seat, uneasiness filled my stomach as I guessed where the story was going.

"The price for her healing was steep, but I could see no other alternative. King Edward said if his healer succeeded, then all he required was my word that one day you would marry his son, Henry. That way our kingdoms could become one, united and strong. I didn't think about the repercussions, didn't consider what might happen if I said yes." He sighed and rubbed his face with his palms before turning back to face me.

"I didn't consider what it would mean for your life to promise you to another without your consideration or consent. Your mother was the only person I thought of. I couldn't lose her."

Father walked toward my mother and placed a gentle hand on her shoulder. Her body shook with silent sobs as she hid her face behind her hands.

"I didn't want you to grow up motherless. I thought I could negotiate with King Edward, thought I'd have time to sort out how to deal with the binding vow I made." His eyes met mine, the anger having been replaced by regret.

"I'm sorry, Sarilda. There's nothing I can do. You must marry Prince Henry in two month's time, or else King Edward will invade and take the kingdom by force. We are not strong enough to withstand his attack. For the sake of our people and your own life, you must marry the prince."

Staring at him, I hugged my arms around my torso as my heart pounded in my ears. My throat ached with unshed tears. I opened my mouth to speak, to say something.

I don't forgive you, but I understand. I wanted to say. *How could you be so brash, so irresponsible? Why didn't you think of me, your only child?* But no words came out.

Without another word, I pushed myself away from the table and rapidly retreated from the room.

Four

I FOUND MY WAY into the garden. The crisp morning air and the bright sunlight were a welcome refuge from the castle walls that seemed ready to squeeze me until I could no longer move.

I wound my way over the paths until I reached the furthest end of the garden, as far away from the breakfast room windows as I could be.

Collapsing beneath the shade of the maple tree grove, I finally let go control and allowed the sobs to leave my body. Tears streamed down my face as I mulled over my father's words, anger welling up in my stomach.

How could you never consider what that promise meant for me? I wanted to scream, wanted him to answer. *How could you be so careless with the life of your daughter and the well-being of your kingdom?*

I hugged my arms around me, leaning against the trunk of the tree for support. *He meant well.* A part of me argued. *He wanted to save your mother, his wife – he acted rashly, but he acted out of love for someone else.*

I shook my head and gritted my teeth. *He may have acted out of love for her, but it was my future that he toyed with in exchange.*

Soon the sobs ceased, my body aching and exhausted from the exertion.

I cannot marry the prince. I must find a way to stop it. There must be a way to change the agreement, to repay the debt without selling myself off and endangering the future of the kingdom. My mind raced with possibilities, wondering what all my father had tried to do to change the agreement and fix my future.

"Have you heard?" A woman's voice drifted through the trees from the other side of the grove. I froze, hoping against all odds that she would turn around. *No one ever comes this far out unless it's necessary.* I thought, wondering why anyone would be in the maple grove this time of year. *It's not time to harvest the sap, and the trees are all trimmed up.* I waited, catching the sound of muffled voices coming nearer.

"What are you chattering on about, Gertrude?" A man's voice interjected. "I thought we were going for a walk – a private walk to be alone." He said, his voice betraying his annoyance as he placed all the emphasis on the word 'alone'.

Ah, I thought. *Makes sense the servants would know this is a more secluded area for some privacy between work.* Blushing, panic brewed that I might hear or witness something I didn't want to.

"We are, Frans." I heard the woman giggle and then shush him and slap his hand. "But this is important!"

Frans sighed. "What is it?" Their feet crunched over the fallen leaves, pausing a few trees away from where I sat, still as stone.

"Well, I hear Princess Sarilda has been promised to Prince Henry."

"That weakling boy who can barely keep his head up?" Frans scoffed in response. "Did he even dance with the princess last night? Why would she go and marry him?"

"Oh Frans, you understand so little sometimes it's almost frightening," Gertrude responded. I searched my brain for a face to match their voices, but none turned up.

I strained my ears for Gertrude's continued explanation as she lowered her voice.

"Whether she danced with him or not, whether she wants to or not, she's going to marry. Royalty don't get to choose who they marry, Frans. It's not like you and me." Another giggle escaped her lips followed by another gentle slap.

"If King Otto tells her to marry the boy, she'll do it. You know as well as I do that the kingdom isn't as strong as it once was. King Edward is a formidable enemy with a vast army. It's a pity the princes all turned to ravens when the princess was born. If it hadn't been for her, King Otto wouldn't be in such a predicament."

I blinked and shook my head, wondering if I'd been hallucinating or if I'd heard her correctly. *The princes? What princes?* The panic rose in my throat once more.

"How is it Princess Sarilda's fault that her brothers were turned into birds when she was a baby?" Frans sounded so offended on my behalf I almost leapt out of hiding. But I refrained.

"Why, if she hadn't been born, King Otto never would have tried to baptize her and the boys would never have gone to get the water. It's her fault they went at all. She's the one the king was thinking of when magic in the kingdom was at its highest. Without her existence, he never would've lost his sons. Which means he would be in a much stronger position now."

"I still say it has nothing to do with the princess. After-all," Frans said, his voice defensive. "She was just a baby. She's not the one who wished they'd become ravens."

An uncomfortable silence ensued. The blood roaring in my ears. *I always wanted brothers.* I thought. *Am I to believe I once had them and they were lost because of my birth?* The idea broke a piece of my heart I didn't know existed.

"Well," Gertrude said, her tone one of offense. "I need to return to work."

Frans did not respond. I waited until their footsteps retreated. I continued to sit in the garden until the sun shone high above and the shade had shifted away from my face, leaving me exposed to the warm autumn sun.

If my brothers are still alive, then maybe there's still hope. I thought, my mind whirring with possibilities. *If I can find them and figure out how to break whatever magic has fallen on them, maybe Father will be able to stand against King Edward. Maybe there's another way out of this ordeal.*

Pushing myself up, I brushed myself off. My head had begun to ache from the tears, the sun, and the lack of food or drink. *First thing's first, though.* I thought, setting my jaw and turning to walk back the way I'd come. *My parents must explain what happened. I need more than the tales of a gossip servant. If this is true and I have any chance of finding my brothers, then I need to understand what happened.*

By the time I returned to the castle, I knew my parents would each be in my father's study, enjoying their midday meal in peace. *Whether they want to or not, they will explain what happened and why I am to blame for my brothers.*

I clenched my fists as I climbed the back stairway to the study.

They'll explain why they never told me about my brothers. I thought. *That's why nothing has been done to save them. Maybe if I can save them, then I can save myself from a loveless marriage as well.*

Five

As I'd expected, I found my parents in my father's study. I stood in the doorway, surveying the scene before me. The midday meal laid out upon the small side table hadn't been touched. My mother sat in front of the fire, staring into the flames.

My father stood at the window, hands clasped behind his back as he glared out at the view of the Sea. If he'd opened the window, he would have been able to catch the faint sound of the waves crashing against the cliffs below.

"Why did you never tell me I had brothers?" I asked, my voice trembling but calm. A sharp intake of air escaped from Mother. Father didn't move. He'd frozen in place, his eyes still fixed on the view outside his window.

"Why did you not tell me I had seven brothers who were turned into ravens? That it was my fault they were turned into ravens? How could you –" My voice cracked and I stifled a sob with my hand.

"How could you keep this from me?" My voice was growing in volume. I pushed into the room, closing the door behind me a little harder than necessary.

"All the times I told you how much I wished I had brothers – or a sibling of any kind – you never said anything. You never thought I deserved to know I once had *seven?*" Tears started to fall down my face as I glanced between my mother and my father.

Mother's body was shaking with sobs, father still hadn't turned to face me.

"Where did you hear that?" Father asked, his voice quiet.

"It doesn't matter, does it?" I retorted, my anger growing. "If it's true, why should it matter how I found out that I had seven brothers who turned into ravens because of my birth? Do you honestly care more about my knowing the truth than about you hiding it from me my entire life?" The idea wounded me more than I thought possible.

Silence ensued as I stared at my father's back. My mother's hand came to rest gently on my arm, but I didn't turn to face her.

"Are you too much of a coward, father, to turn and tell me the truth?" I asked, knowing my accusation would get the reaction and response I so deeply desired.

He turned to face me, his eyes piercing my own as he seethed with indignation. He opened his mouth to speak, a fiery urge to defend himself driving him. But the fire left his gaze before the words could leave his mouth.

His shoulders slumped forward and his face dropped. A hand went to rub his forehead as he closed his eyes and sighed.

"What happened?" I whispered, turning to face my mother. "What happened to my brothers?"

"It wasn't your fault." My mother whispered between sobs, tears streaming down her face. "You did nothing wrong. You were a baby." She squeezed my arm and pursed her lips.

"When a child of royalty is born, magic in the kingdom of Eryas grows strong. Stronger than any other time." She lead me toward the chairs in front of the fireplace and sat me down opposite the one she'd occupied a few moments before.

"You were such a wonderful, unexpected gift." She said, smiling down at me through her tears. "We were all so excited. We'd wished for a daughter for so many years. When I became pregnant with you, we hoped and prayed to the gods that you might be a girl."

"A week after you were born, when the kingdom was still brimming with magic, the priest told us to fetch water for your baptism." She wiped a stray tear from my cheek and sat down in her chair. "So we could name you and celebrate your birth." Her voice faltered, as though she were trying to find the right words to explain what happened next.

"I sent your oldest brother to fetch the water." My father interjected, coming away from the window to stand beside my mother. "His name was Peter." His voice cracked as he spoke the name.

"I told Peter to go fetch water from a nearby spring, one where the fairies like to make their home." He said, his eyes growing distant. It was as though he could no longer see me.

"The other boys found out where Peter was going, and they all decided to go along. They were so excited about their little sister, about your birth and baptism. They didn't want to miss out on the fun." He paused, considering his next words.

"What were their names?" I asked, folding my hands into my lap as I steadied my voice.

"There was Peter, of course," my mother picked up where my father left off, reaching up a hand to grasp his own. She smiled slightly, a sad smile. "Then Alexander, Wolfgang, Andreas, Johann, Friedrich, and Ernst." Her voice cracked again.

They both sat in silence for a moment, their gaze distant, their hands clasped in the other's. I gave them a moment then leaned forward to touch my mother's knee. She started, as if she'd forgotten I was there.

"What happened when they went to fetch the water?" I asked, resting my chin in the palms of my hands as I waited for them to answer. My mother turned away, her hand dropping from my father's as she brushed away a new stream of tears.

Father cleared his throat. "They left early in the morning," his voice was unnecessarily high-pitched. "By mid-afternoon, we began to grow impatient. I sent a servant after them to make sure they were alright, to get them to hurry along and bring back the water for your baptism."

My father frowned and stared down at his hands, clenching and releasing his jaw as he spoke the next few words. "The servant came back a half hour later soaked to the bone. He said he'd found them playing in the spring. When he tried to tell them to move it along, they grabbed him and threw him into the water, laughing and pointing.

"He swore he tried for a good ten minutes to get them to come back with him, but they wouldn't listen. They were so enthralled with their play in the water that the baptismal pitcher had fallen in the spring and sunk to the bottom. He brought it back with him and gave it to me."

My father turned and walked back to the window, leaning against it with one arm. "I lost my temper." He whispered. "Standing in my throne room, looking out the window in the direction of the spring, I lost my temper and cursed my sons.

"Without thinking about the magic in the land or what I held in my hands, I asked that my sons might be turned into ravens. The next thing I saw was seven ravens taking flight from the trees." His voice was a whisper, so quiet I had to strain my ears to hear him.

"It's not your fault, Sarilda. There is no one to blame but myself."

Sitting back in my chair, I tried to process what I'd been told. My mother continued to cry in her chair. She'd shrunk in her grief, becoming somehow smaller than before. My father continued to stand beside her, leaning against the chair for support.

"How old were they?" I asked, unsure of why I cared.

"Peter was fourteen." My mother replied. "Ernst had just turned seven." Her voice shook. "You were our miracle child, the daughter we never dreamed we could have. Now you're our only child, and your destiny is no better than that of our sons." She cried harder, sniffing into a handkerchief she'd pulled out of her sleeve.

"If they were still here, if they were still alive as boys – as men – would you be able to stand against King Edward?" I asked, my mind whirling with possibilities.

"They're not." My father replied, his voice tight.

"But if they were," I said, standing up and turning to face him. "Would you be able to stand against King Edward? Would you be able to make him listen to reason and accept a different repayment for his service?"

Father turned to look at me, and I dared him with my eyes not to answer my question.

"Yes." He said, nodding. "If your brothers were still alive, still here in the kingdom, I would not – that is, you would not be in danger."

I searched his face for a moment, considering everything I'd learned, then turned to leave. Pausing, my hand rested on the door handle.

"I will not go quietly to my doom." Not looking at either of them, I took a deep breath. "I will find a way out of this. We have eight weeks. I will fight to find a way forward every day until that time is up."

I didn't wait for my parents to answer.

Six

I spent the rest of that day wandering the gardens and the woods. By nightfall I found myself sitting on the shore, staring out at the saltwater.

No one had come looking for me. Not even Captain Bastian. It seemed everyone had been informed of my future and instructed to leave me be.

My stomach rumbled with hunger and my head ached with thirst. I refused to go back to the castle. It felt more like a prison now and less like a home.

They didn't even try to break the curse, to find my brothers. The thought came back to me on repeat, causing my eyes to burn with unshed tears. *Why wouldn't they try to find them? Try to save them from a life they didn't deserve?* I'd never been angry at my father before. Annoyed? Yes. Angry? Never.

He was always ten feet tall, invincible, and kind. I thought, staring out at the moons rising as the sun disappeared beneath the horizon. One small, one large, both bright and full. I'd always thought of my parents when staring at the moons keeping watch over Eryas.

Father was always king, wise, and wonderful. How did I not see who he is at his core? The word "coward" tumbled around in my mind. *Prideful, unwilling to admit his wrongs. He would rather see me carted off like a common criminal to pay his debt than to admit to the kingdom – and to himself – that he's the one at blame.*

Soft footsteps approached behind me. "Leave me be, Mother," I said, not bothering to turn around. She ignored my comment and came to sit beside me.

"I thought I might find you here." She said, adjusting her skirts as she looked out over the sea. "This was always your favorite spot to sit and think, even as a little girl." Waves lapped at the shore below as an owl called to us from a nearby tree.

I'd expected her to nag me, to tell me to stop being childish, to go home and eat something and go to bed. But to my relief, she did not.

"If I'd never overheard about my brothers," I said, not daring to look at her. "Would you have ever told me the truth?"

"No," she said, her voice soft. "I don't suppose I would have." She didn't hesitate, didn't turn away or make excuses. Something about her truth-telling acted as a balm to my wounded heart. "That would have been wrong, but it's what I would have done if you'd never found out."

I wanted to ask her why, but that suddenly seemed unimportant in the face of such genuine honesty.

"Did you ever try to find them? To bring them home and break the curse?" I asked, unable to keep the accusatory edge out of my voice.

"No," she answered. "Your father wanted to, but I fell ill soon after your brothers disappeared. He was distracted." She paused, reaching out to take my hand between both of hers.

"We always thought the boys would come back to us somehow. They flew away, we figured they would fly back." I let my hand lay limply between her own, allowing her to stroke it as she spoke.

"It was wrong of us, Sarilda. By the time we accepted they weren't coming back, you were already two years old. It seemed pointless to even try." Her voice shook as she spoke, and she cleared her throat. "Surely after two years they'd been killed or had died, or simply did not remember who they were. Where would we have started our search?"

She paused, still stroking my hand. "We chose you, Sari. We chose to spend our days raising and training you."

I shook my head and pulled my hand away from her, a bitter laugh escaping my throat. "No, Mother," I said, rubbing my face and turning to meet her shocked eyes. "Don't try to lay this on me. You chose yourselves."

Mother turned away, her cheeks red with shame. "I'm sorry." She whispered, wrapping her arms around her knees, and leaning forward. "You're right."

"I'm going to find them, Mother," I said, watching as she began to rock herself back and forth. "We have eight weeks before King Edward comes to collect or kill. I'm not going to sit around and wait for my life to be over." I waited for her to object, but she didn't.

She continued to rock back and forth; her eyes fixed on her knees.

"I'm going to find my brothers, break the curse, and bring them home." I stood up and brushed off the sand and dirt from my clothes. My head pounded as I rose, but I managed not to stumble. "Either I find them, or I die trying," I said, turning to walk back through the woods. "Don't tell father. He'll try to stop me." I said over my shoulder, taking a few steps toward the trees.

"Sarilda," Mother called after me. I'd reached the edge of the path. Pausing, I turned around to face her. "I will not try to stop you," Mother said, moving toward me. "And I won't tell your father, but you must promise me something before you go."

I nodded in acknowledgement of her request, unsure if I would be able to promise her anything.

"Promise me you'll come home, even if you can't find them. Even if you become mortally wounded." She came close and held out a trembling hand. "Even if you refuse to marry the prince and choose to fight King Edward," Her eyes brimmed with tears as her hand remained outstretched, waiting for me to grasp it. "Please come home."

I considered denying her request - thought about how absurd it would be for me to promise something so completely outside my control. But before I knew it I'd reached out to grasp her hand in mine, my heart softening as she swallowed back the tears.

"I promise," I whispered, squeezing her hand. In an instant I was in her arms, gathered up in a tight embrace.

"Then go, my darling." She whispered into my ear before kissing my cheek. "Go now before I change my mind. Go find your brothers and bring them home." Her voice cracked and she released me.

Leaving her at the edge of the woods, she watched me walk into the darkness of the trees. When I reached my room, I found a tray filled with food and tea. I devoured the food, chugging the lukewarm tea before going to the basin of water and drinking half of it down.

Ringing the bell for my handmaiden, I asked her to bring me more bread, cheese and fruit, and another pot of tea. Her eyes grew wide, but she obeyed without question.

While I waited for her to return, I threw a change of clothes and an extra cloak into a pack. Rolling up one of my warmest, but lightest blankets, I secured it tightly to the bottom with twine.

Just as my handmaiden knocked, I threw the pack under the bed. I thanked her for the food and dismissed her, shutting and locking the door from the inside as she retreated.

I wrapped the food in cloth and packed it at the top of my bag, filling one bottle with tea and another with the rest of the water. Surveying my pack, I tossed a small bag of coins I had into the bottom of it.

Securing my cloak around my neck, I pulled on my bow and arrows, strapping my throwing knives and sword around my hips.

"Sarilda," I heard my father at the door, a tentative knock accompanying his voice. "I'd like to talk." He jiggled the door handle, letting go as he realized it was locked. "Please open up."

I didn't answer. Instead, I snuffed out my lamp and sat on my bed in the dark, waiting for him to leave. My heart pounded in my ears as I considered what I would do if he called for a servant to open the door. After a few moments his footsteps retreated, and I breathed a sigh of relief.

I waited in the dark, staring out my window at the moons as they rose high in the sky, listening to the seconds on the clock tick by. I was exhausted. But sleep did not come for me.

In the wee hours of the morning, I unlocked my door and crept down the servant's staircase to the kitchen.

Cook sat beside the dying embers of the fire, her gentle snores rising with each breath. The outer kitchen doorway sat cracked open. Crossing the room, I eased the door open and slipped through, pulling it back behind me. It never made a sound.

Seven

T**he cool fall air** hit my face as I exited the castle. The scent of fallen leaves and dew-covered earth filled my nostrils. The kitchen garden led out to the woods on the north side of the castle.

Leaving the rocky path, I crept along through the long, decorative grass lining either side of the path. My leggings were soon soaked from the knee down, causing a dull chill to run up my body as my feet went numb, but I hurried on.

As I reached the woods, I turned back to catch a final glimpse of the castle, realizing it might be the last time I saw my home. *I have no idea where I'm going,* I thought, aware of the fact that I'd never travelled any further than the neighboring village.

This is foolishness. I should turn back and go to bed now before anyone wakes up. I can find another way to save the kingdom, to keep from marrying a prince I do not care about.

My brain urged me to return the way I'd come, but my feet remained glued to the forest floor and I leaned against a nearby tree for support.

This may be foolishness, but it's the only chance I have at finding my brothers, saving my kingdom, and maintaining my freedom.

I turned and continued in the direction of the spring where my brothers had turned into ravens and disappeared. Leaves crunched underneath my feet, twigs snapped, and the distant chatter of night owls met my ears.

The moons were bright, casting their cool light through the almost barren trees. Soon, I reached the spring and paused to look around.

Water trickled through dark rocks, landing in a pool that held it until the overflow ran through a small stream that trickled south-east. *Where do I go from here?* I wondered to myself, refusing to give way to the doubt creeping into my mind.

Who do I ask for directions? How do you even begin to search for seven brothers you've never met who turned into ravens when you were a baby and flew away from here?

The question sounded ridiculous. *I was so ready to escape, so sure of myself that I could save the day and find them.*

Now that I'm here, I don't know what I'm supposed to do. A twig snapped on the other side of the pool.

I froze, sucking in my breath as I stared into the darkness, my hand perched on the hilt of my sword. Shadows moved, but I couldn't tell if it was my eyes playing tricks on me as branches swayed in the breeze.

There is no breeze. I thought, realizing I'd created an excuse for something I didn't want to be real.

"Who's there?" I said, my voice hardly above a loud whisper. "Show yourself," I demanded, summoning all my courage to face whatever might emerge from the darkness of the trees.

A light flickered. I squinted, raising my hand to shield my eyes. Soon, the light morphed into a face, leading to the body of a small woman with intense eyes gazing at me from across the water.

I stared in wonder, captivated by the bright blue of her eyes. Her white hair was piled in a mass of braids all over her head with flower crowns pinned about haphazardly.

Her dress was unlike any material I'd ever seen before, shiny and soft, flowing around her as though by choice, changing from color to another with each blink of the eye. In her right hand she held a glowing light, illuminating the area around us. Her pale skin shone like diamonds, as though reflecting the light she carried in her hand.

"This is no place for a princess." She said, her voice gentle as the words drifted over the pool in my direction. "You should be in bed, safe in the castle. Not out here in the woods with no one to care for you, to protect you."

Is that a threat? I wondered, unable to tell if her words were meant to be kind advice or something much darker.

"I'm sorry." I stammered, trying to decide what the best course of action would be. "I didn't mean to disturb you. I'll leave now if you can point me in the right direction." I ducked my head in an effort to show deference.

She tilted her head to one side, a smile spreading across her face. "You're sorry?" She asked. "For what? You haven't done anything to me, my dear. Why would you leave?" She took a step forward, stopping next to the pool as she continued to hold up the orb of light in her hand and stare at me.

"Are you not the Princessof Eryas?" She asked, frowning at me as though she were displeased. "Did you not come from that castle at the edge of the woods?"

I nodded, unable to form words.

"What is it you seek, child?" She took a step forward, and then another. I gasped, expecting her to sink in the water. But her feet merely rested on the surface of the pool beneath them. She smiled again. "Why did you come to this spring?"

I cleared my throat. "Yes, my name is Princess Sarilda." I said, the words hesitant as my voice cracked. "Please," I said, watching as she continued to approach. "I'm looking for my brothers."

She stopped, as though taken aback by my words. Stepping forward, I paused beside the pool.

"When I was a baby, they came to fetch water for my baptism. My father became angry when they did not return quickly, and he cursed them. They turned into ravens and flew away." *Why am I telling her all this?* I wondered as I spoke, the words coming out awkwardly, sounding too loud in the presence of the still pool. "Can you tell me anything about them?"

I waited for her to answer, watching as she regained her composure and took a few more steps in my direction. She was so small, her head barely as high as my chest.

"I do indeed know of your brothers and the fate that came upon them." She said, softly. Her eyes met mine, as if searching for something. "I would be lying if I said I didn't have a part to play in the magic that granted your father's wish." Her voice trembled as she spoke and her eyes grew distant, losing a bit of the spark they'd maintained since the moment I met her.

"I waited many months for someone to come looking for them," she said, breaking free of whatever memory had transported her to the past. "I waited for someone to ask how they might break the curse." She paused, searching my face. "No one ever came. No one ever bothered to check." Curiosity lit up her eyes, accompanied by sadness.

I paused for a moment, expecting her to tell me where to search. "Well then?" I said, impatient for answers. "Where are they?"

"If you desire to find your brothers and break the curse that binds them, it can be done." She said, tilting her head as she continued to study me. "But it will only come at great personal cost to you. The magic that bound them, while foolish, is strong.

"It will not be easy to find them, and I cannot guarantee you will find them in time to save your kingdom." She paused again, watching to see how I would react to her words. "My question for you, Princess Sarilda, is how much are you willing to sacrifice for brothers you've never met?"

Staring down at the strange little woman in front of me, my mind raced with fear, doubt, and absolute resolve warring within my stomach. I jutted out my chin, and straightened my spine as I shifted my pack.

"Where are my brothers?" I asked, this time my voice was firm and steady, loud enough to be heard. "Please, if you know anything, if you have any idea where they might be, tell me where to go."

A smile broke over the woman's face. "If your brothers are still alive, and my light tells me they are, you will find them if you follow the river to World's End."

I blinked and stared at her. "World's End?" I asked, unable to hide my incredulity. "Is that a joke?"

"It's a city, child." She laughed, throwing her head back as laughter escaped the depths of her belly. "I will lead you to the river crossing where you can book passage on a boat. At the end of the river, atop the great waterfall overlooking the same sea you have looked out at your entire life, you will find the great city, World's End."

"Are my brothers there?" I asked, my heart pounding so loud within my chest I could hear it. "Will I find them in the city?"

"That I do not know and cannot promise, my child." She reached up and touched my cheek lightly with her free hand. A warmth spread over me, and I realized how chilly and stiff my legs had become. "But I can promise you will find your way to them if you follow the river to World's End."

I studied her for a moment, relishing the warmth that had filled my cold limbs. "Show me the way to the river."

Eight

I FOLLOWED THE WOMAN through the woods for hours, her glowing orb guiding our way through the trees. She walked much faster than I expected, never hesitating on where to turn.

By the time the sun began to peak through the trees, the chill of the nighttime dew had overtaken the feeling in my limbs once more. Yet, somehow, I was sweating from the exertion of our steady pace.

I heard the river before I saw it, the muffled calls of boat hands drifting through the trees. The woman's orb still glowed, but its light was faint, as if the emerging sun beckoned it to fall asleep and rest. She stopped abruptly beside an oak tree and beckoned me to stand beside her.

"See that?" She said, pulling down a branch for me to peer out at the scene behind the cover of trees. "That boat leaves as soon as the sun has fully risen. You must be on it.

If you're not, I'm afraid King Otto and his men will catch you before you have a chance to reach World's End."

Men bustled around the boat tied to the dock at the edge of the tree line. The water flowed steadily, not rushing or dwindling. The boat was unlike any I'd ever seen.

I'd grown used to the majestic wooden ships that sailed past our shore and the small boats they used to row between where they dropped anchor and where they disembarked on our shore.

This boat was larger than those used to come ashore and smaller than any ship. A small mast set in the middle of the boat held a sail that had been secured for docking, and a large oar sat on either side of the boat.

In the bow was a platform, with what appeared to be a small room underneath. In the stern was another, a little bit taller than the one in the bow.

Like a miniature ship. I decided, unsure what else to make of the floating thing before my eyes. Five men bustled around the dock and the boat, while an older man sat on a stool shouting instructions and insults to the rest.

"How do I get on? Do they take passengers?" I asked, my eyes still fixed on the scene before me.

Two of the men were dragging heavy barrels onto the boat and storing them inside the room beneath the platform over the bow.

Two others had stopped what they were doing to take a drink from a water bucket beside the man.

Another had climbed up the small mast and seemed to be checking the sail. I thought about the small amount of money I carried on me, wondering how long it would last if my journey to World's End led me somewhere else.

"Yes, child." The woman said, her voice calm and quiet. I could feel her eyes burning into the side of my face. "I would advise against offering them money in exchange for your passage. The last thing you should do is reveal who you are."

Turning to look at her, I wondered if she could read my mind. "Then how am I supposed to get on that boat? Why would they let me on at all?"

Her eyes lit up and she cocked her head to one side. "See how the old man sits on his stool and never raises a finger to help?" She said, pointing at the scene through the branches. "Do the others appear particularly happy with him?"

"Of course not," I replied, irritated at the question. "They look like they'd rather throw him in the river than listen to him give out orders."

"Exactly!" She hissed, barely containing the laughter I knew was trying to exit her mouth. "This is where a little bit of mischief might come in handy."

Before I could respond, she pulled the glowing orb close to her, whispered something to it, and blew in the direction of the dock. A fluttering light drifted from the orb, through the branches, and down toward the dock.

I watched, unsure if I should be impressed, excited, or horrified.

"What did you do?" I asked, my eyes fixed on the men as the light settled over them, unnoticed.

"Watch and see, my child. Always watch and see."

The two men carrying barrels glanced at one another, set down the barrel near the middle of the boat, and stomped back to the dock, their eyes locked on their target.

The older man wasn't paying attention to them, he was shouting at two of the other men struggling to unload wooden crates from atop the platform in the stern. They cursed as the bottom of the crate they were carrying collapsed, all of its contents spilling out over the dock.

"Why you useless, good-for-nothing, lazy-" The old man was on his feet, raging at the two as they tossed the wooden crate aside. They tried to scoop up the contents that had spilled out into a pile.

"I'll hold you personally responsible for any damage, I will!" He screamed, shaking his finger in their direction. His wide-brimmed hat was tilted just right so that he couldn't see the barrel carriers stalking toward him.

A mix of delight and horror filled me as the two picked up the old man. They grabbed him underneath either shoulder, and tossed him into the river - hat, and all. I clamped my hand over my mouth as a shriek of laughter rose in my throat.

The old man's hat floated down the river as he popped up from the current, gasping from the cold air. Within a few seconds he was swimming toward the shore as the five men on the dock clapped and wheezed with laughter.

"Now's your chance." The woman hissed at me.

"I don't understand," I replied, turning to meet her eye with confusion and humor splayed across my face. "How is this supposed to help me gain passage on that boat?"

"Child, who is more likely to help a poor girl down on her luck? Men angry with each other for what they're doing – or failing to do – or five men who've just had a laugh at the expense of someone who wasn't helping them?"

"So," I said, glancing between her and the men. "I'm supposed to walk down there and *ask* them to let me ride on the boat?" I couldn't contain my continued incredulity.

She nodded, her bright blue eyes glinting in the light of the rising sun as it pushed through the withering leaves hanging onto the branches above. "Yes and offer to work for your passage."

"What if they say no?" I said, my pulse pounding in my neck as my feet remained frozen to the ground where I stood. "What if they get angry or recognize me somehow?" I hated the fear coursing through my veins, the way I wanted to run home and admit defeat.

I don't even know my brothers. I don't know if the curse that binds them can be broken. Why am I doing this? The thoughts wouldn't stop, the doubt and the fear tumbling through my mind as I considered doing exactly what the woman told me to do.

A soft, warm hand landed firmly on my arm, causing me to look down and meet her eye. The warmth from the night before spread through me once more, cold drifting away from my limbs like it had never clung to me.

"If they say no," she said, her face more serious than I'd seen it before. "If they recognize you, or attack," she leaned in, pulling my arm so that my face came level with hers. Her bright eyes burned into mine, unblinking.

"Then you fight with all the skill and training you've been gifted. You fight until they admit defeat. You fight until they yield." She let go of my arm and patted my cheek. "I'll be right beside you, child. Don't you worry."

I nodded, straightening as courage flooded through me. "Thank you." I said, a small smile spreading over my lips. The woman nodded and motioned for me to go.

"Don't thank me yet, child. I believe you are the only one who can undo the curse your father spoke over your brothers. As I said before, it will come at great cost to you. Thank me when your journey is complete."

I inclined my head to acknowledge her words, unsure of how to respond. Taking a deep breath, I pushed through the trees and into plain view of the men.

The five men were still laughing, bending over, and wheezing. They gripped their stomachs and their knees while the old man continued to scream and curse at them.

NINE

THE MEN'S LAUGHTER DIED out as they caught sight of me. I felt a surge of anxiety but pushed forward. *It's too late now. If I turn back and run they'll run after me and wonder why I'm acting strange.* I tried to form a pleasant but stern expression on my face and pushed back the hood of my cloak, blinking as sunlight hit my eyes.

"Good morning, gentlemen," I said, forcing confidence into my voice and thanking all the gods I'd heard of that it didn't shake. "I see you've had a bit of, uh, misfortune." My mouth twitched as I chose my words carefully, directing them toward the older man. The five younger men relaxed and smirked.

"What do you want?" The old man hissed at me. He'd pulled off his jacket and boots, and now stood wringing out the shirt he wore, trembling. It was hard for me to tell if he trembled from cold or if rage alone made him shake.

Swallowing, I wet my lips, forcing a weak smile. "I wish to trade service for a ride on your boat. I must reach World's End, and I've been told that's where your ship is heading." I glanced around at the five men, all of whom traded glances before looking me up and down, sizing me up.

"We don't need any help." The old man said, hopping on one foot as he pulled off a sock. "And if we did, why would we take you?" He glared at me as he switched feet, his hair dripping in his eyes.

"I know I'm thin, but I'm strong," I said, squaring my shoulders. The closer I'd gotten, the shorter I'd realized he was. "I'll work hard for my passage, and I'll keep to myself."

"No chance." The old man said, throwing his socks on the dock. "We don't need y-"

"Shut up, you old blow hard." The man who'd climbed the mast yelled and shook his head. "Why anyone can see she's more fit to make the trip and stronger than you are." He turned to smile at me, kindness lighting up his eyes.

"But I must ask, miss, what takes you to World's End? A great city it may be, but not one where I'd send a young woman all alone…" His voice drifted off and he shook his head again, as if he were unsure of how to explain his reasoning. The smile on his lips transformed into a frown.

"I am of age, sir." I said, trying to keep the flush of embarrassment from my face as I searched for the answer that might convince him to let me go. "My reasoning is my own, but I swear I would not go if it were not a good one." I matched the intensity of his gaze and stood my ground. He studied me for another moment, his eyes wandering over the weapons and pack I carried.

"I do not mean to pry." He said. "The gods know I have secrets of my own I do not wish to share with complete strangers." He hesitated before turning to look at the other four. "What say you, lads? Shall we let the lady on our boat?"

To my surprise, they all nodded, smiles breaking over their faces as well. All but the old man who stood there, trembling, and sputtering his disapproval.

"Can you cook, miss?" One of the men who'd been carrying barrels asked, unmistakable hope in his eyes.

It was my turn to smile. "Yes, I can. I've been told my cooking isn't half bad." I said, my shoulders relaxing a little.

He grinned back at me. "The name's Jack, miss. That's Ian," he said, pointing to the man who'd climbed the mast. "Then Jacob, Henry, and John." He pointed at the remaining three. "Oh, and that's old Silas." He said, his lip curling as he pointed at the old man. Turning back to me, his smile returned. "And what should we call you?"

Opening my mouth to answer, I hesitated before pushing forward. "Sarah." I said, my stomach doing a somersault as I realized how close I'd come to spilling my real name. "My name is Sarah." I said.

"Sarah?" Ian said, unconvinced I was telling the truth. "And where did you come from, Sarah?"

My palms began to sweat, and my mouth went dry. *I should've known I'd be asked questions like this. I should've come up with a story before I left the shelter of the woods.*

"Oh, leave her alone, Ian." Jack said, pushing the man as he spoke. "What difference does it make to us where she came from? The sun has almost risen, and we haven't even finished loading the boat. There will be time enough for questions later." He winked at me, a wink that implied I shouldn't worry about those questions ever being asked again.

"Besides," he folded his arms and looked me up and down once more. "What danger could she possibly pose to us? No offense, miss." He added, quickly. "I dare say you're a good fighter and you look strong enough, but you're just one person."

No one responded to him, not even Ian. I waved my hand, trying to appear to dismiss his remarks.

"Jack's right," said the man I believed was Jacob. He was shorter than the others, with a stout build, dark beard, and dark eyes. "We're wasting daylight. If she wants to come with us, I see no harm. Leave her alone and let us be on our way. We're due to arrive in World's End day after next. If we take any longer to set sail, we'll never make it in time. Grand Master Dietrich will fine us and refuse to do business with us next time."

Ian gave me one last hard look as I waited with bated breath, my feet frozen and my hand twitching over my blades. Then he shrugged his shoulders and turned back to the barrels. Soon I was helping load the last of the crates, securing them safely on the platform over the stern.

As Jack unfurled the sail, Silas stood next to the rudder in the stern, a blanket wrapped around his still-trembling frame. The other four took their positions at the oars and the boat began to drift down the river.

The morning sun warmed me through as I sat near the bow, studying the tree line for one last glimpse of the woman. A gentle light bounced from behind the branches, mixing with the bright sunshine. Smiling to myself, I wondered if I'd ever see her again. *Farewell you strange, wonderful woman.* I thought, wishing I could raise my hand to say goodbye. But I resisted as more than one pair of eyes watched me where I sat.

A wonderful sense of calm washed over me again and I closed my eyes, leaning back against the side of the boat. *When was the last time I slept?* I wondered, realizing how heavy my body felt and how dry my eyes had become.

I pried my eyes open and glanced around the boat. The four men rowed along, humming a tune I'd never heard before. Ian caught my gaze with a quizzical expression, but I turned away and forced myself to look at Silas.

The old man stood with a sour expression on his face, barefoot and still draped in a blanket. He glared at me then looked back at the horizon.

Finally, my eyes fell on Jack, who stood next to the sail, tweaking it as we went along. He grinned at me and nodded, closing his eyes. A sense of relief washed over me.

They don't need my help. I can sleep. It's okay. I smiled, grateful for his kindness, leaned my head back once more, and drifted off to sleep.

TEN

I WOKE WITH A start, drawing a knife from my belt and pushing it against the throat of the man fumbling with the pack beside me. I shoved him to the ground before he could retaliate. He froze as I blinked, struggling to focus my eyes in the bright midday sunlight.

"Sarah, don't." A man's voice said. *Sarah?* I thought, confusion washing over me. *Right, I'm Sarah.* Memories from the morning came flooding back. The woman in the woods, the boat, Jack, Ian and the others. Silas being thrown into the water. My eyes focused on Ian's face.

"Why are you going through my things?" I asked, my voice hoarse and my breathing labored. I didn't back off but fixed him with a look that I hoped communicated how close I was to slitting his throat.

He let go of my pack and raised his hands over his head in a sign of surrender. "I meant no harm." He said, his voice calm and collected.

"That doesn't answer my question," I said, applying a bit of pressure to my knife. "I may be outnumbered, but I would rather die on this boat and take you with me than back off now."

Ian grinned. "I would rather live and let live." He replied, not moving. "I was only trying to find out more about you. I did not mean to frighten you, and I meant no disrespect."

"Sarah," Jack was the one speaking. He took a tentative step forward. "Let him be. I swear it won't happen again. Will it, Ian?" He addressed the man beneath my knife, his tone filled with annoyance.

"Won't happen again." Ian replied, still not moving.

After a second more, I backed off and pushed myself up, sheathing my knife, but keeping my hand poised to withdraw it if necessary. Snatching my bag up, I tightened it.

"If it does happen again," I said, looking from Ian to Jack to the others as I set the bag down where I'd been asleep moments before. "I won't ask questions." I looked back at Ian. "Do we understand one another?"

He pushed himself up, dusted himself off, and nodded. "Absolutely."

Not like I have anything in here to give me away. I thought, processing what had happened as my stomach began to growl. *But the last thing I need is someone stealing what little I have or thinking they can pry without consequence.* Relaxing my hand from the knife at my side, I turned to Jack.

"What do you need me to do?" I asked.

Jack tilted his head to one side and folded his arms across his chest. "I think a meal would be nice." He said, his eyes lighting up. He nodded toward the barrel stove near the bow of the boat. A small stack of wood sat beside it, two pots and a large pan stacked on top of it. "You'll find the food in the storage room of the stern, along with fresh water."

I forced a smile to my face and nodded. "No problem. I'll have some food ready within the hour." Hesitating, I grabbed my bag. "Anything special you'd like me to make?" I offered, trying to extend the olive branch.

Jack's gentle smile spread across his face. "Anything you care to make will be better than what we'd be eating if old Silas were doing the cooking." He winked and turned back to the sail.

I glanced at Silas, who glared at me in return and curled his lip as he muttered something under his breath. He'd removed the blanket and his clothes had dried in the bright sunshine. Sweat trickled down my back, making me realize how warm it had gotten beneath the fall sun.

Setting down my bag next to the woodpile, I removed my bow and arrows, unclasped my cloak, and piled it all neatly together, my bag at the very bottom of the pile.

Rolling up my sleeves, I built up the fire in the barrel and grabbed a nearby bucket and empty basket.

To my relief, the storage room door didn't have a lock on the outside. All it had was a simple latch.

At least they can't lock me in. I thought. *However, I'll still leave it open and move quickly.* I swung open the door and pushed a stray piece of firewood against it before entering.

The storage room was cold. The sweat on my skin cooled and a shiver ran down my back. Blinking, I allowed my eyes a few seconds to adjust to the lack of sunshine.

I found the water barrel near the door. Filling the bucket, I ventured deeper into the dark room.

Through the light of the open door I managed to pick out a few potatoes and carrots. An onion, a bundle of dried herbs hanging from the ceiling, and a bag of thick salted and dried meat soon joined the rest.

Throwing the food in the basket, I carried it and the bucket of water back to the door and stepped out. The sun hit my eyes, making me squint. I glanced over at my pile of goods. It appeared to be untouched. *Good.* I thought, relieved.

The next half hour flew by as I boiled water, diced vegetables, and threw everything together in the larger of the two pots. As soon as the vegetables softened, I tasted it and called the men over to eat.

One by one they filed over, taking turns eating the stew. Jack went to the storage room and brought out a loaf of bread, tearing it into pieces and handing us all a chunk.

Jack, Jacob, Henry, and John all smiled and thanked me as they devoured the stew, leaving their bowls stacked beside the stove to be cleaned up.

Silas came next, glowering every step of the way. He gave no thanks, but his eyes lit up as he ate my stew and soaked his bread in the leftover broth.

Finally, Ian approached, bowl outstretched, eyes wary. I filled his bowl without a word and turned away to fill mine.

"I meant no harm, miss." He said, his voice quiet. "I just wanted to find out more about who you might be. You didn't tell us much."

"You're not very good at apologies," I replied, my eyes fixed on my bowl. "Besides, if I wanted to hurt you, I would have already. Why do you need to know more about me? No one else in your party seems to care. What's it to you who I am or why I'm heading to World's End?" I turned to face him, folding my arms over my chest, and ignoring the sweat dripping down my brow.

He studied me, one hand holding his bowl, the other clutching his bread. "I meant no harm."

"Why don't you tell me what you were looking for in my bag, and I'll tell you if it's in there." I offered, surprised at myself.

He clenched his jaw and turned away, stalking over to the other side of the boat to sit down.

I ate alone, my growling stomach savoring every last bite of food as I realized I hadn't eaten since the night before. Chewing, I tilted my head back in the shade.

What will I do when I get to World's End? I wondered. *Who will I ask? Where will I find information about my brothers?* I sighed. *No time to think about that now. All I need to do right now is clean up the dishes.*

Pushing myself up, I made quick work of the dishes. By the time I was done, Jack asked me to help with the sail.

The rest of the afternoon slipped by uneventful. I longed for the sun to disappear behind a cloud, or down the horizon. Its relentless beating made me groggy and sluggish. Soon it was time to prepare another meal and the men were pulling up the oars and tying up the sail.

The sun disappeared as we all ate supper together around the stove. The boat drifted slowly down the river of its own accord.

As the moons rose in the sky, John and Jacob broke into song and Jack and Henry pulled out pipes to smoke. Silas retreated to the stern of the boat with the same sour expression on his face he'd had all day, settling down by the rudder. Ian stared at the firelight leaking out from the stove. They'd all indulged in a glass of beer, and Jack's jolly demeanor had only improved.

"Tell us a tale then, Ian." Jack said, elbowing the other man out of his reverie.

Ian started at the mention of his name. I expected him to be annoyed, but he didn't seem to mind. Leaning forward, he rested his chin in his hand.

"When I was a young boy, my father used to take me down the river once a year to visit World's End. He wanted me to learn the trade." He paused as he opened the stove and pitched in another small log. "One day, as we were settling in at the dock, we heard a great commotion overhead." I felt my heartbeat quicken as I began to suspect where his story was headed.

"When I looked up, the outline of seven ravens – the most enormous ravens I've ever seen – crossed before the setting sun, crying as they flew. They were headed in the direction of World's End, following the river as they flew."

I stared at Ian, my mouth dry, my stomach tight.

"So?" Jack asked, confusion on his face. "What of it? Ravens fly together all the time."

Ian looked up to meet his gaze. "I've never heard them cry like this before. My father swore and told me only dark magic could be involved in such an event." He shifted his eyes to meet mine. "Magic that was running rampant in the land because of the birth of the princess."

A chill spread over me. I wanted to look away, but all I could manage was to pull my cloak tighter.

"That was the day the seven princes of Eryas disappeared," he said, still staring. "The day the princess is said to have been baptized."

"You mean to say you believe the princes turned into ravens?" Jack said, his voice incredulous. "Why?"

Ian continued to stare at me as he spoke. "Some say an evil witch turned them to ravens out of spite. Others say King Edward had something to do with it. Still others," he hesitated, as if regretting what he was about to say. "Others believe the princess herself cursed her brothers."

"That's ridiculous." I snapped, the words leaving my mouth before I could stop them. Everyone turned to stare at me, their glossy eyes and relaxed faces sobering. Closing my mouth, I stared into the fire, unsure of what to do next.

Jack cleared his throat. "They've never been found, have they?" He turned back to Ian. I could feel Ian's eyes fixed on me.

"Not yet." Ian responded. I didn't look up. My eyes remained glued to the flames like my life depended on it.

An awkward silence ensued in which I could feel the eyes of every man in the group shifting from me to Ian and then to Jack.

Why did you open your mouth? I scolded myself. *Why couldn't you just stay quiet for once in your life?* I prayed the rest of the men didn't suspect what I assumed Ian did.

"Well, I think we should get some sleep," Jack said, clearing his throat and pushing himself to his feet. "Old Silas has first watch at the rudder. Sarah," he paused and looked around. I turned to meet his eyes. "You can have your pick of where to sleep. I swear no one will bother you or your things." He said.

I nodded, grateful for his guarantee. "I'm good here," I said, gesturing to the stove. "If that's okay with you?"

Jack nodded in return and started to walk away, all but Ian following his lead. "Aren't you coming, Ian?" He asked, obvious concern in his voice.

"In a minute." The man replied.

"See that it is only a minute."

Jack retreated, the others following behind him, and my heart beat faster the further away he went. They disappeared into the room beneath the stern, Silas glaring after them as he sat at the rudder.

"I know." Ian whispered. I felt as though I'd been punched in the stomach, the air slipping out from my lungs. Turning, I met his gaze. "I know." He repeated. He didn't smile or glare or betray any specific emotion.

What does he want from me? I wondered, my mouth dry. Before I could respond, he stood and retreated to the room beneath the stern.

Eleven

I SPENT THE NIGHT staring at the barrel stove and drifting off to sleep then waking in a panic.

Each time I woke to Ian's dark, intense eyes boring into my own only to realize it was a dream. The men took turns at the rudder throughout the night, all but Ian and Jack.

As the sun rose, everyone exited the room beneath the stern and shuffled around the deck, readying themselves to row once more. I realized it was time I made something for breakfast.

Pushing myself up, I put a pot of water on to boil and took the basket back to the storage room, propping the door open as I had before. My eyes adjusted to the dark space. I found a loaf of crusty bread, a bag of tea, more dried meat, and a sack of oats. As I scooped out a large cup of oats, the doorway darkened behind me. I turned instantly, dropping the food without hesitation.

"What do you want?" I hissed. Ian's outline was all I could see, his face hidden by shadow.

"The truth." He replied.

"The truth?" I scoffed, curling my hands into fists. "You already know the truth. I'm Princess Sarilda, searching for her long-lost brothers who were turned into ravens the day of my baptism."

"Why didn't you tell us you're the princess?" he asked, his voice low. He leaned against the door frame, crossing his arms in front of his chest. "Why keep it a secret? We would've helped you."

I swallowed. "How was I supposed to know that? How was I supposed to know you wouldn't betray me and take me home or - worse yet - hold me for ransom?" I hesitated before proceeding. "Did you tell the others?"

I waited for his reply, hoping against all hope that the answer would be no.

"Why would I tell them something they care nothing about?" He waited for me to answer, but I didn't have one. "Jack probably suspects. But he minds his own business. He has no reason to get involved. Old Silas may be a grouchy old fool, but he wouldn't sell you out. The others will do as Jack, and I tell them."

Processing everything he'd just said, I stood there. "What are you going to do now?" I asked, letting out a sigh. "I don't have much money, and I didn't bring any valuables other than my weapons, and a change of clothes. I can't afford to pay you very much for your silence or your help." I kept waiting, trying to make out his expression in the dark.

"I don't want your money." He said, offense obvious in his voice. "But if you would like my assistance, then I'll do what I can to help you once we reach World's End." He turned to leave.

"Why?" I asked, taking a step forward. "Why are you offering to help me?" He froze in the doorway but didn't turn around. *What is wrong with you, Sarilda?* I thought, appalled at my own insolence. *Why would you ask such a question?* I couldn't find an answer.

"I had a sister once." He said, turning slightly. "She was born the same year as you, but her lungs were weak. She died before her first birthday." The soft grief in his voice dredged up guilt I'd never known. "If I could, I would search for her until I found her, and bring her home. I can't do that. However, I can help you find your brothers if they're still alive. I can help you bring them home."

"What was your sister's name?" I asked, realizing I'd taken another step closer, my hands and shoulders relaxing.

"Anabella."

"That's a beautiful name." I paused for a second, swallowing as I reached a decision. "Thank you, for your offer. I accept."

Ian nodded and retreated without another word. After a moment's pause, I picked up the basket, gathered my ingredients, and got to work cooking breakfast.

That day passed quickly, as did the next night. I slept hard, exhausted from the previous nights of little to no sleep, and the constant beatdown of the Autumn sun.

When the sun rose on the third day, I could see the outline of a city ahead of us, other boats also coming into view as the river widened.

As we drew closer to the city, I stood at the bow in awe of the sight before me, my mouth gaping like a child in a candy store.

World's End lived up to its name at the end of the river, at the edge of a waterfall, where the fresh water rushed into the saltwater sea below. Massive stone walls, hewn from surrounding rocks, rose before me, creating a walkway over the river that hustled and bustled with the sounds of a busy market.

Two iron gates had been drawn up, allowing entrance to boats. We floated through without problem, but I felt the eyes of a dozen hidden soldiers watching us as we found an empty dock.

The water was swift, pulling us in the direction of the closed gates at the other end of the enormous inner compound. Beneath the sound of haggling and arguing from the humans above, I could hear the dull roar of the waterfall.

I stared at the four walls surrounding me, towers rising from four corners, blocking out the sun. Dozens of windows punctured the stones, laundry strung from one to another, walkways crisscrossing overhead. The crew docked their boat before I realized what had happened.

"It's really something, isn't it?" Jack said, coming to stand beside me, breaking the trance that seemed to have befallen me. I nodded, sparing him a quick glance before returning to my sightseeing.

"If you don't close your mouth soon," Ian said, coming up on my other side. "You'll catch a fly."

I shut my mouth and turned to glare at him, but my glare melted away at the amused grin on his face.

"Don't listen to him," Jack said. "We all reacted the same way the first time we came here. I suppose we've grown used to it all."

Laughing, I turned in a circle as I tried to continue taking in my surroundings. "I've never seen anything like it. Do all these people live here?" I asked, the sheer volume of people shocking me as they continued to go about their business.

"Not all," Ian said, hoisting a sack onto his shoulder. "But most. Some are like us; they travel here to sell their goods. Speaking of which," he nodded down the dock. "Grand Master Dietrich is waiting. Let's go collect our pay."

I turned to search for the man who'd hired them. At the end of the dock stood a stout man in a bright scarlet coat, and navy-blue pants. His coat had been decorated with golden threads stitched into an intricate design of leaves. He wore knee-high black boots that had been recently shined.

On his head sat a wide-brimmed navy hat with white feather plumes cascading over it like a waterfall. In his hand he held a black, curved cane that seemed to be more for show than it was for balance. A sour expression covered his face, on par with the one Silas wore. It was framed by trimmed and curated facial hair rather than the scruff of a river sailor.

Jack and Ian approached, each bearing a sack of goods on one shoulder. They exchanged a greeting.

Two men, cowering as they moved, took the sacks from my companions while the Grand Master stood by, unmoved. He looked inside each sack, pulled out a handful of grains, then nodded in what I assumed was satisfaction.

The two cowering men shouldered the packs and disappeared into the crowd. The Grand Master withdrew a small satchel from his breast pocket and deposited it into Jack's hands. Jack opened the satchel, peering at the contents, then nodded in approval and turned back to the boat, Ian following behind him.

I found myself staring into the eyes of the Grand Master as he caught sight of me watching them. His expression changed, a frown forming in his eyebrows before a sneer rose along his upper lip. Flushing with embarrassment, I turned away and gathered my things together. His eyes continued to follow me as I tried not to glance back. I offered to help them unload the cargo, but Jack smiled and waved me away.

"Go explore, take care of the business you came for." He paused what he was doing and looked around at the bustling dock. "The city is safe during the day. As long as you keep your wits about you, you should be fine." He stepped a little closer and lowered his voice, frowning.

"Unless you have somewhere to stay, please know you're welcome to come back and stay with us until tomorrow. We leave at dawn, but you are always welcome on our boat, Sarah." His lips twitched as he spoke the name I'd given him. "Be careful." he said, extending a hand and ducking his head.

I smiled and shook the hand extended to me. "Thank you, Jack. I will." I turned and looked around for Ian, only to find him standing at the end of the dock, waiting for me. Grand Master Dietrich had disappeared.

That's a relief. I thought. Shouldering my pack, I walked toward Ian.

"Do you have a plan?" He asked, his voice just loud enough for me to hear. "Do you know where to go or who to ask for information about your brothers?" He was leaning against a post, catching his breath. Sweat dripped down his forehead and neck. His eyes darted around, but his face remained as relaxed as if he were discussing the weather.

I hesitated before shaking my head. "I was hoping you might have an idea?" I admitted, trying to smile as I adjusted the pack on my shoulder and shifting my weight from one foot to the other.

I assumed maintaining a relaxed expression on my face might be a good idea.

"If anyone knows about your brothers, if anyone remembers, I have a feeling it would be the Sacred Order of the Sun." He took out a scrap of cloth and wiped his face. "They live in the city monastery. They've been here for decades. Go there, ask to see their council of elders. They might know something about your brothers."

He paused and looked around before taking a step in my direction and lowering his voice even more.

"Be careful, princess. Jack is correct in saying the city is safe during the day. But World's End is a treacherous city, a last stop for many fleeing the rule of your father. I do not say that to offend," he added, holding up his hands as I felt myself surge with a desire to defend my father. "Only to warn you. I have no feud with your father. But many do – right or wrong."

I nodded, swallowing down the words of defense that had pushed up my throat. "If the monks don't have the information I need," I said, glancing around. "What do I do?"

"If the monks don't know, come find me. I'll be here. As Jack said, we don't sail until dawn tomorrow. You should have plenty of time to ask them."

"Thank you, Ian," I said, smiling again and extending my hand. "For everything."

He nodded with a smile of his own, squeezing my outstretched hand. "Be careful." Before I could reply, he turned and walked back to the boat.

Twelve

I wandered through the streets, stopping to ask vendors if they could point me in the direction of the monastery. Some refused, telling me to buy something if I wanted directions, but I was loathe to give up any of my coins yet.

After a half hour of wandering, I stumbled upon a loan monk standing at a street corner. He stood there, chanting with arms outstretched as he turned his head toward the sun.

His head was shaved bare, his skin withered and tan from years of exposure. The wrinkles covering his thin face made it difficult for me to guess his age. He was clothed in a loose, brown robe tied at the waist with a bit of rope. A hood fell across his back, attached to the robe, and his calloused feet were clad in sandals.

"Pardon me." I said, when he paused his chanting and lowered his arms. The man turned to look at me, crossing his arms in front of him and bowing in my direction after a quick glance up and down. I took this as encouragement to continue.

"I believe I'm looking for your monastery. Would you be so kind as to show me the way when you're done here?" I fumbled over the words, trying to show my appreciation for any help he'd offer me, while also hoping he would be done soon.

"What business would a fine young lady like yourself have at the monastery, miss?" He replied, eyeing me with surprise. "If you don't mind me asking."

I hesitated but moved closer and hoped no one around us would notice. "I need information about a lost family member," I said, deciding it would be better to tell a fib now and the whole truth later. "Someone told me they came this way many years ago, and that the monks might know something about them." I waited, searching his face for any sign he might do as I was asking.

After a moment's hesitation and another glance up and down, his face broke into a gentle smile and he nodded. "I was just finishing up." He said. "I have one more chant to offer up to the sun goddess, and then I'll take you to meet with the elders." He bowed again, beckoning for me to stand to the side. "If anyone knows where your family member headed after coming here, they are as good a place to start as any."

Returning his smile, I stood off to the side while he delivered his chant, watching the passersby. No one paid either of us any heed. The crowd seemed immune to his presence, as if they'd heard his chant a million and one times.

I'd chosen to shrink into the shadow of the nearby wall, which made my presence much less intrusive.

After what felt like an eternity, but in reality, was probably only a half sandfall, the monk lowered his hands and his face once more. Pulling on his hood, he turned to me with a smile, and waved for me to follow him.

We worked our way through the streets at an even pace. People moved out of the monk's way as though he were diseased, but never turned to meet his gaze.

That's odd. I thought, trying to understand if it was awe or fear that caused everyone to scurry out of the path of a single oncoming monk. They sent sideways, curious glances my way. But every time I tried to meet their eye for some hint of information, they looked away.

The city never ceased to amaze. I passed over bridges, walked down steep staircases, through inside hallways, and back out to more bridges. Up ahead, a whitewashed building shone bright in the noonday sunlight.

The wooden doors were open, but the dark inside of the building seemed to dare anyone to enter. The monk disappeared inside, waving at me to follow once more. Slowing my pace, I took in the sheer height of the building towering over me.

Soon the doorway enveloped me. I blinked, but did not slow my pace, listening to the soft footsteps of the monk ahead of me.

A light appeared up ahead and I found myself in a bright courtyard with a clear pool of water at the center. I stopped short, taking in the deep green of the ivy that covered the whitewashed walls and the fading purple flowers blossoming along it.

On the other side of the courtyard sat another monk, cross-legged and perched on the edge of the pool. His hands were folded inside his sleeves, his hood had been cast back to embrace the streaming sunlight, and his eyes were fixed on the water before him. Much like the first monk I'd met, his head was shaved, his skin tanned, and his age impossible to guess.

I waited as the first monk walked around the pool toward his companion, bowing deep a few times but never pausing.

"Brother Cristofer," the monk beside the pool said, his tone gentle and smooth. "You bring a visitor I had not expected to see. Not in my lifetime, anyway."

Brother Cristofer bowed once more, pushing away his hood as though it annoyed him. "Brother Samuel," he began. "This young lady found me as I went about our sacred chants to the sun goddess and requested my help.

Am I to understand you already know who she is?" He glanced from the monk to me, curiosity splayed across his face.

The monk laughed and looked up from the water at me. "Yes, I saw her as she sailed upon the river. The sun goddess showed me in a water vision during my meditation these last three days that she would be coming."

I stared in disbelief. "You saw me?" I said, meeting his gaze. I wasn't sure if I should be thankful or frightened. "Do you know who I am?" I asked, hoping it didn't sound as though I expected him to but that I was surprised he did.

"Yes, little sister." Brother Samuel laughed again, his eyes crinkling at the corners. "The goddess has told me a great deal about you and your mission. Tell me, how did you find the light witch, Ryna?" He tilted his chin back, eyeing me as he spoke. "Many moons have passed since I had the pleasure of meeting with her."

My mouth fell open before I could stop it. "She never told me her name." I stammered, well aware that was not an answer to his question.

"You never asked, now, did you?" He said, his warm laugh growing a little louder.

"If you please, Brother Samuel," Brother Cristofer interrupted. "She came to ask the direction of the elders. If the sun goddess has chosen to bless you with a vision of her quest, perhaps you might provide the answers she seeks?"

"Indeed, brother! I plan to!" Brother Samuel exclaimed, his hands coming free of his sleeves as he swiveled around and stood up, leaning heavily against Brother Cristofer as his legs buckled beneath him.

Has he been sitting there for three days? I wondered, unsure of what to think about the idea of the sun goddess showing him a vision, surprised by how quickly I accepted his words.

"But first," he continued, turning to look at me and waving for me to walk around the pool and join them. "It's been three days since my last meal, and a full night since my last drink of water."

I started around the pool, telling my feet to move from where they'd frozen in place.

"Would you do us the honor of joining us for a meal, Princess Sarilda?" Brother Samuel asked. Brother Cristofer looked startled as he heard my name, but his surprise was soon replaced with a smile as he continued to support the unsteady monk beside him.

I nodded, offering a hand to help steady him. He shook his head and did not take my offered hand. "No offense, Your Highness, I appreciate your desire to help. It is against my vows to touch a woman unless it's an emergency, or a healing of the sun goddess demands it of me. My devotion – body, mind, and soul – is to her alone."

I lowered my hand, embarrassed even though I knew nothing about this strange cult of monks. "My apologies," I said, unsure of how else to respond.

"Come!" He replied with another smile. "Let us eat together and I will give you the information you seek. That is," his smile faded a little and he looked away. "I'll give you the information that has been revealed to me."

I nodded again, understanding his meaning, but unsure of what I was about to learn. My stomach rumbled as I followed the two monks through another archway, a long corridor, and into a room with a vaulted glass ceiling and wooden tables all around.

Ivy grew along the iron holding the glass together, its purple flowers still strong in the warmth of the room. I pushed back my hood and stared.

Nothing at the castle compares to this room, not even the ballroom. I thought, the bright sunshine and purple flowers soothing a piece of my soul I didn't know existed. Tears formed in my eyes as I considered the beauty of the room.

Brother Samuel had regained the majority of his balance, standing off to the side as I took in the room. Other monks bustled about, pausing to look me over before moving on with their meal.

"Come, little sister." He called to me, pointing to a bench at the table. "Sit and eat. We have much to discuss."

Thirteen

"Your brothers did, indeed, come toward World's End after they were cursed by your father." Brother Samuel said, ripping off a piece of bread and dipping it into the bowl of creamy mushroom soup before him.

A large wheel of cheese, mugs of cider, crisp apples, and several types of butter, jam, and honey lay before me. I devoured the food, my mouth watering with each bite.

"Do you know where they are now?" I asked between mouthfuls, hope rising in my chest. "Did the sun goddess tell you where they might be?" I took another drink of cider and wiped my mouth with the linen napkin set beside me.

"The water vision sent to me by the goddess revealed their passage here, as well as their continued journey." Brother Samuel said, smiling at my use of the sun goddess's title.

"Their continued journey?" I asked, my heart sinking at the words.

"Yes," he said, his smile turning sympathetic and his voice lowering. "Unfortunately, they are not here in World's End. They stayed for many years, building a nest at the top of one of the towers and stealing food from vendors and sailors alike." He paused to take a bite of an apple.

"But Grand Master Dietrich drove them away after receiving multiple complaints." His face soured as he spoke the Grand Master's name. I bit back the tears threatening to fall.

"I see," I said, staring at the remaining food on my plate. "Did she tell you where they went?" I asked, trying to brace myself for what I believed was the inevitable bad news.

"She did." He said. I turned to meet his eyes, hope rekindling. "Have you heard of our holy land?" He asked, dipping another piece of bread in the soup and slurping it up. "It lies to the East, named Sun City."

Flushing with embarrassment, I realized how little I knew of the world outside the palace. "I'm afraid I don't," I admitted, my voice quiet as I dipped my spoon into my soup and took a bite.

"Well," Brother Samuel said, unphased by my ignorance. "You'll have a chance to see it now. As that is where your brothers headed after they left World's End."

I nodded. "I would be honored to see your holy land," I said, not meeting his eye. "But do you know if my brothers are still there?" I couldn't help asking, hating that I did.

Brother Samuel hesitated before responding. "That's where the vision grows blurry. I am sorry, little sister. I cannot guarantee they will still be at City of the Sun when we arrive." He paused and took another bite of his apple. "However, I know you'll be headed in the right direction. I believe it's your best chance of finding your brothers before the clock runs out."

The reminder of the ticking clock was one I had been loath to keep at the front of my mind. "I understand," I said. "How do I get there?" I turned to look at him, sure that my face showed the defeat I felt.

He grinned and folded his hands together to rest his chin, his green eyes glinting in the sunlight.

"You are welcome to travel with us tomorrow." He said. "For you have arrived in time for our annual pilgrimage to the Holy Land. We leave at dawn from the Eastern gate. Will you accompany us?"

Hope fluttered inside me as I considered his generous offer. "I can pay you," I said, pulling out my small pouch of coins and pushing it in his direction. "It's not very much, but I can pay you as thanks for your assistance."

To my surprise, he frowned and pushed the coins back, shaking his head. "Little sister, that is not necessary." His tone was grave. "You are our guest in need of help. Your payment is not required. Please, keep your money."

As I picked up the coins and pocketed them, I had the distinct feeling I'd offended him. "I did not mean-" I started, but he held up a hand and shook his head.

"All is well. I know you meant no harm." His smile returned, and my shoulders relaxed. "Will you go with us, then?" He asked once more.

"Gladly and with thanks," I replied. "If you'll still have me."

"With pleasure," he said, leaning forward and lowering his voice. "Your Highness." The smile spread from one side of his face to the other and he returned to his meal.

"Finish up your food and I'll show you to a guest room." Brother Cristofer said, startling me. *I'd forgotten he was here.* I nodded.

"Thank you."

My room was small and simple, but warm. A window took up the entirety of the outside wall, a thick curtain slung across it for privacy.

Setting down my things, I perched on the side of the bed. The curtain had been pulled back, allowing for the late afternoon rays of sunlight to stream in through the window.

What do I do now? I thought, staring out at the sunlit courtyard from my perch on the bed. *It's too early to go to sleep. But what else is there to do?* I thought back to the boat, to Ian and Jack and the crew.

Maybe there's enough time for me to say goodbye, to let them know I found someone to help me. Leaving my bow and arrows on the bed, I took only the knives strapped to my waist. I pulled up my hood and descended to the courtyard.

"Where are you going?" Brother Cristofer's voice stopped me dead in my tracks. I turned to face him. He was standing in a ray of sunshine in the corner of the courtyard, head bare, arms outstretched.

"Not far, I just want to let someone know I'm okay. I'll be back before it gets dark."

He frowned but nodded. "Be sure you do, little sister. It's not safe to wander the streets of World's End alone at night." He paused and shifted from one foot to the other. "Especially for someone like you."

"I promise, I won't be long," I said, smiling beneath my hood and turning to leave. He didn't respond, but I could feel his eyes following me as I disappeared into the dark corridor that led to the street. Once outside, the noise of the crowds picked up.

I glanced around to catch my bearings, found a sign pointing the way to the docks, and followed it. I wound my way down staircases, over bridges, and through crowds that all seemed hell-bent on walking in the opposite direction of whatever way I needed to go.

It's getting dark. I realized unease starting in my stomach as I neared the docks. It had taken me longer than I'd expected to reach the boats. I could see the boat up ahead, bobbing softly on the water. The laughter of the crew reached my ears and I felt a sudden pang of sadness. *I will never again have the opportunity to sail with them or listen to their stories in front of the warm barrel stove.* The thought crushed my heart.

Maybe this is a fool's errand. I thought. *Maybe I should give it up, go get my things, and come back to join them on the boat. I could still escape the marriage.* The idea made my blood rush as I thought about sailing up and down the river.

But then my people would suffer. My parents would die. My brothers would still be lost. The excitement vanished as quickly as it had arrived. *Don't be silly, Sarilda. Go tell them you're safe and get back to the monastery. You're wasting valuable time, you fool.*

"Where do you think you're going?" A harsh whisper reached my ears, causing me to freeze in my tracks. I turned to search for the owner of the voice but found no one.

"Who are you?" I responded, not bothering to whisper back. My hands were poised to throw a knife if necessary. "Show yourself."

A small form emerged from the shadows, clothed entirely in black. "My name matters not." The voice hissed. The creature's face was hidden in the dark. "I serve Grand Master Dietrich." It took a step toward me. I held my ground.

"We've been waiting for you to return. We had a feeling you might come back." It cackled. I turned, realizing five more creatures, identical in size and clothing, had emerged from the shadows around me. I could hear my heart pounding in my ears.

"What do you want with me?" I asked, working hard to maintain my calm. "What does Grand Master Dietrich want with me?"

The creature cackled again. "Why, to give you over to King Edward, of course." He took another step and pointed at me with a long, gloved finger. "Or hold you for ransom to your weakling father." I glanced around as the lot of them advanced on me. The sun had disappeared from the street I was on, leaving only shadows.

"Now why don't you make things easy on yourself, and come with us without a fight?" I turned back to the creature as he pushed back his hood.

Blinking, I took in his horrifying features. His skin was green, his ears long and pointed, and his eyes were red. An evil grin spread across his face as he continued to come closer. I'd never seen a goblin before.

"We swear we won't hurt you. Well," he said, pausing to consider what he'd just promised. "We won't hurt you much." He cackled again, the gleam in his eyes like something from a nightmare.

Without another word, I decided to attack first. I pulled a knife in each hand and lunged. The Goblin's eyes bulged with surprise before his lips curled in a snarl.

Dozens of sharp fingernails clawed at my back as the other five attacked me from behind. I cried out in pain but did not stop. Throwing a knife, I nicked his right ear. He howled and snarled, a gloved hand reaching up to inspect his wounded ear.

"You'll pay for that!" He screamed and lunged at me. I threw my second knife, pulling another from my belt as I tried to throw off the goblins on my back.

From the corner of my eye, I saw movement on the docks. Then, to my surprise, I felt the goblins being wrenched off, one at a time, shrieking in horror as they ripped skin from my back.

The goblin in front of me howled as a knife lodged in his foot, pinning him to the ground. I turned to see Ian running toward me, another knife in his hand.

Turning around I found Brother Cristofer standing over the crumpled bodies of the goblins who'd attacked me from behind, a sword dripping green perched in his hand.

"You?" I stammered over the screams of the goblin trying to free himself of the knife. "You followed me?" I asked, unsure if I was grateful or annoyed.

"When you did not return," he said, reaching down to wipe his blade on the cloak of a dead goblin. "I came to find you. I told you, little sister, the streets are not safe." He sheathed his sword and his hands disappeared into his sleeves as he waited for my reply.

"Sarilda?" Ian said, coming up behind me. "Are you alright?" Turning back, I watched as he grabbed the goblin from behind and pulled the knife out of his foot.

The goblin shrieked again and tried to claw his way out from Ian's grip. But he soon realized it was no use and chose to hang there, growling.

"I'm alright," I said, surprised not to feel more pain. "I'm sorry," I said, looking between Ian and Brother Cristofer. "I shouldn't have come. It's just…" Words escaped me. "I'm sorry," I repeated, staring down at the ground.

"No harm done." Brother Cristofer's gentle voice came closer. "Except for your back, little sister." He said. "We should get back to the monastery. Brother Samuel can treat your wounds."

I looked up at Ian, nodding my agreement with Brother Cristofer. "I wanted you to know I'm safe," I said, realizing how silly it sounded after the danger I'd faced. "I didn't want you to worry." I shrugged.

Ian's face held a mixture of amusement and fear.

My eyes settled on the goblin. "What will happen to him?" I asked, frowning, and searching for the knives I'd thrown.

There was a moment of silence as Brother Cristofer and Ian seemed to consider my question. I located my knives, cleaned them off on the cloaks of fallen goblins, and sheathed them.

"He'll crawl back to his master." Brother Cristofer said, nodding at Ian to release the prisoner. Ian hesitated a moment, then released the goblin.

"You'll regret this." The goblin snarled, pulling up his hood and limping away. "Grand Master Dietrich will not be pleased."

"Away with you then." Brother Cristofer said as Ian brandished a threatening knife. The goblin disappeared without another word. "We should go before he returns with more friends." He said to me, then turned to Ian. "I would advise you push away from the dock for the night. They'll not venture into the water."

Ian nodded his understanding and took a step toward me. "Please be careful, princess." He whispered. "Our offer still stands. You are welcome any time. Please realize there are those in our world who want to hurt you. Be on your guard. Stay close to the brothers."

A sense of foolishness overwhelmed me like a child being rebuked. But I couldn't object. I knew he was right. I nodded and turned to leave with Brother Cristofer.

Fourteen

Brother Samuel treated my wounds with hands so gentle I barely felt his touch. He dipped a clean cloth in a mixture of something I did not recognize and laid it gently across the puncture wounds from the goblin claws as I lay on my stomach in my room. The warm liquid settled over my back, soothing the non-stop stinging.

My eyes soon grew heavy. He covered me with a thick blanket, blew out the candle beside my bed, and closed the door behind him as he left.

I slept hard that night, my dreams a constant haze of seven ravens crying out my name. I felt no distress, only confusion.

I don't know where to find you. My inner voice would try to tell them, my lips unmoving as I watched them. *I'm trying, I promise. I will do everything I can to save you.*

The morning dawned sooner than I wanted, but I rose, packed my things, and exited my door just as Brother Cristofer came to get me.

He led me to the dining hall, where we ate a hurried breakfast of thick porridge sweetened with honey. We drank large mugs of tea accompanied by fresh bread with butter. The sun streaming through the windows above us warmed me to my core, waking me up.

Before the sun had risen, we were gathered at the Eastern gate. Brother Cristofer, Brother Samuel, and five other monks surrounded me. Raising their arms to the sky, they threw back their heads, allowed their hoods to fall over their shoulders, and chanted a prayer to the sun goddess.

I stood in the middle of them, unsure of what to do. A small audience looked on, whispering about the strange young woman accompanying the monks.

As soon as they finished, Brother Samuel turned to me, smiled, and began to walk North, following the river. We walked in single file, Brother Cristofer bringing up the rear. We took with us no pack mules, nothing but what we could carry.

The monks each held an ornately carved staff in one hand. A sword was strapped to their left side beneath their cloak, and they shouldered a pack of blankets, water, food, and cooking utensils. I'd been given a couple of canteens to add to my load, but nothing else.

As the day wore on, the heat picked up and the route changed. We slowly veered further away from the river, its calming sound still within earshot, but no longer visible as we headed East.

By the time we stopped for the day, the scenery had also begun to change. The lush green trees and high river grass gave way to a dry wasteland with withered oaks and sandy pits.

That night the monks took turns keeping watch as the rest of us slept around a steady fire. In the distance wild dogs howled, my heart racing at every sound around me.

If I strained my ears, I could still hear the river, but I knew it would be gone by the time we stopped again the next day. My sleep was fitful, visions of seven ravens circling me from above haunting my dreams.

The night grew cold, a piercing wind picked up from the North and rushed over the barren, dry land. It shook the withered trees as it tried to pierce through my blankets and clothing. Without the warmth of the fire beside me and the watchful eyes of the monks, I wondered if I would've survived the night.

I was exhausted and relieved when the sun peaked over the horizon. Packing up my things, I happily prepared a meal of porridge while the monks performed their morning ritual together with their faces uncovered before the sun.

"What was out there last night?" I asked Brother Cristofer as he came to grab some porridge. "I mean, other than the wild dogs. I felt like there was something surrounding us." He gave me a weak smile and lifted an eyebrow.

"That depends on who you are and what you believe." He replied, spooning up some porridge and blowing on it before putting it gingerly in his mouth.

"What do you mean?"

"Some say the lost souls of those who have died on this journey haunt these lands." He said, shrugging his shoulders as he looked around us. His voice was hushed, a sense of respect in it. "Others believe the wild dogs are the reincarnation of those lost, and the creatures you sensed are spirits from another realm."

I shivered, not from the cold, but from the ideas he presented. "What would the spirits want with us?" I asked, not sure I wanted to know.

He turned, his eyes meeting mine. "To feed on your soul, on the life that runs through you. They are the reason souls are lost in this land to begin with. Unless you know your way, and are strong of faith, you can easily be led astray on this journey and consumed by the darkness." He took another bite and looked around again.

"Long ago, the sun goddess fell in love with the spirit of the oak tree. They pledged their love forever and a day. This land was once as green as that along the river, as lush as the woods that border your castle."

"But after a thousand and one years, she discovered he'd been unfaithful to her. She found him with the spirit of the river. As her heart broke, her anger burned. She could not stand to have reminders of him within her borders. So, she burned away each oak tree, and sucked dry the land of all water to keep away the spirit of the river. Then she told the spirit of the oak tree to never enter her lands again."

I stared at a nearby tree, one that had creaked the night before in the wind. "Are you saying, the spirits of these trees are what haunt this land with the wild dogs?" I asked.

Brother Cristofer shrugged his shoulders again and took another bite. "It's impossible to know for sure. At the end of the day, it matters little who they are, and it matters much that we do not fall prey to them."

"How do you serve a goddess who admits to destroying innocent life as an act of revenge on her lover?" The words came out of my mouth before I could stop them. I stared at Brother Cristofer in horror. "I'm sorry, I shouldn't-"

"No," he interrupted, raising a hand to silence my apology. "It's a valid question. One I'm sure many in World's End would like to ask us if they dared to do so." He smiled.

"The sun goddess does not mind questions; she will not punish you or me or anyone else for asking questions. Neither does she promise to answer them." He said with a pointed look. "I do not follow the sun goddess because I understand everything she has done or will do. I follow her and pledge myself to her service because that is my calling, and I believe her to have my best interest at heart."

I pondered his answer for a moment, watching as he finished his porridge and cleaned out his bowl.

"Tell me, little sister," he said, setting down the bowl and spoon next to the fire to dry. "What is your calling?"

My heart beat faster and louder, thudding in my ears. "To find my brothers and save my people from an invasion, I suppose," I said, trying my hardest to instill a sense of calm and security in my voice.

"Do you understand all of your calling? Is there nothing you still question? Nothing you still seek to know?" He was staring at me, searching my face.

"No," I replied, looking down at my hands. "I don't understand. In fact, I'm not sure I believe my calling." I admitted, hating every word.

"Take heart, little sister," Brother Cristofer whispered, kneeling to catch my eye. "Neither do I." His smile widened. I nodded, wishing I could hug him, but refraining out of respect for his vows.

"Time we were off." Brother Samuel said, coming up to us, staff in hand.

He looked happy, but tired, as though he hadn't slept well the night before. "We have much ground to cover before nightfall." He hesitated a moment, staring at a spot on the ground. "I fear tonight the spirits will be more active than last night. We must be on our guard."

"When will we reach Sun City?" I asked, standing to grab my things. Shouldering my pack made me wince, but the pain in my back soon dissipated.

"Day after tomorrow, little sister," he said, smiling. "No need to fear. Only be on your guard." He looked around. "I've made this journey once a year for the past thirty years. The spirits have only succeeded in stealing away my companions once." His face fell as he spoke. "I do not expect or intend that to happen again. Not if we all take courage and stay alert." He turned away and beckoned us to follow.

We were soon all walking again, in single file, into the dry wilderness beneath the ever-warmer sun. We slowly moved further East, and the sound of the river disappeared completely. No matter how hard I tried, I could no longer hear its gentle flow.

The land beneath my feet grew softer and sandier with each step, and the withered oak trees grew scarce. The sand turned into soft dunes, making each step more labored as I began to climb up and down the small hills.

By the time we made camp that night, I was a sweat-drenched, exhausted mess. I shoved the food given to me into my mouth and drank my portion of water.

Falling into my blankets beside the fire, I tried to ignore the wind sweeping over the dunes and the growing sound of howling dogs.

The monks took turns, two at a time that night, guarding the camp with their eyes fixed on the dark dunes. They kept their staff grasped in one hand while their sword was grasped in the other.

As tired as I was, my sleep was fitful, and I woke more times than I could count. The howling became deafening, the wind picked up speed.

My sweat turned cold beneath my blankets, refusing to dry for most of the night. My body ached, and my back stung. Beneath the unending noise, I could hear Brother Samuel whispering prayers from his bed roll.

No one will sleep tonight.

Fifteen

By the time Sun City came into view, my back had somehow stopped stinging, but every part of my body ached. I stood beside the monks as they performed their chants, raising their arms to the continuous sun with uncovered heads.

Multiple domed towers and long stretches of wall rose from the dunes, glinting gold in the bright sunshine. A massive gate that appeared to be open sat in the middle of the towers.

I squinted, my eyes aching from the bright light. *Are those helmets?* I wondered, unsure if I was seeing soldiers or if the sun was just playing tricks on my eyes.

"Come, little sister." Brother Samuel interrupted my thoughts, his voice weak. "Let us descend to Sun City before nightfall." I turned to meet his bloodshot eyes.

Too much sunlight and too little sleep. Not that he would ever agree he'd been exposed to too much sunlight. I thought, wishing I could do something to help. He was breathing heavily, a light cough beginning in his chest.

I managed a weak smile. "I would be happy to descend to your sacred city with you," I said, nodding my agreement. An eager smile spread across his face, like that of a little boy about to show his friend a new toy.

In a single file, we descended the dunes. Each step made it harder to tell exactly how far we had yet to travel. By the time we reached the gate, we were all breathing hard. Brother Samuel leaned heavily on his staff, and Brother Cristofer had left his position in line to walk beside the older monk.

Panting, I stared up at the massive towers, the sun at my back as it began to set. The walls shimmered like gold, but I could now see the soldiers I'd suspected were there.

Two guards at the gate towered over us, their shining armor glistening in the sunlight. Brother Samuel came to a halt as the guards each held up a hand for us to stop.

"State your purpose, brother." The guards said in unison. Their voices held no emotion, their eyes drifted over our group and landed on me before shifting back to our fearless leader.

"I come, as always, to worship the goddess and bask in the light of her glory." Brother Samuel said, bowing his head. His voice was hoarse, and he was leaning on his staff with both hands. "I believe this will be my last journey in this life before I ascend to serve the goddess in the next world."

"Why do you bring with you an unbeliever?" The guards replied, glancing back at me. My stomach tightened into a knot as my fist tightened around the sword at my side.

Brother Samuel frowned and straightened slightly. "Since when are those in need turned away from the gate of the sun goddess?" He asked, his tone pleasant, but somehow still challenging.

"By whose authority do you question our discernment?" He continued. "Little sister poses no threat to our people. She simply seeks answers that lie within these walls." He beckoned toward the open gate. "Answers the goddess herself has shown me." The last words were as calculated as an answer can be.

I wasn't sure if I should be grateful for Brother Samuel's words or if I should tell him to shut up. The guards stared at me for a moment without looking at Brother Samuel or any of the other monks.

"Very well." They said in unison. "She may enter, but only if she goes directly to the temple to speak with the High One."

They turned back to Brother Samuel. He nodded and moved forward; Brother Cristofer close by his side. I followed behind them, my hand still perched over the hilt of my sword.

The city towered over me, still glistening in the fading sun behind us. *What must it look like in the morning?* I wondered, fully expecting I would be required – not just invited – to see the sunrise. I looked up at the rod iron gates as we passed beneath them.

Once inside the city I looked around for any sign of life, but only a few people walked the streets. All of them were monks, dressed much the same as my companions in their brown robes.

The only sound on the streets was that of a low hum as those who ventured outdoors chanted quietly to themselves.

Brother Samuel stopped as we reached what looked to be the center of Sun City, leaning heavily on his staff. "I fear I do not have the strength to accompany you, little sister, to see the High One."

Brother Cristofer and another monk closed in beside him, taking his staff away and positioning themselves underneath each arm to steady him. I stood in front of him, wishing I could reach out and squeeze his hand, hating how hard I had to fight to refrain from touching him as worry grew deeper inside me.

"I will send you with Brother Cristofer," he said, a feeble smile crossing his lips. "I must rest." He paused, turning to nod at Brother Cristofer as another monk took his place. Brother Cristofer let go reluctantly and came to stand beside me.

"If the High One allows, come and say your goodbyes before you depart." Brother Samuel continued. "It has been an honor to serve you. I know the sun goddess chose to shine her favor upon you. I will pray for your success in finding your brothers until my dying breath." He bowed his head slightly, the circles under his eyes growing darker as his head dipped down.

"Thank you." I managed, wishing to say so much more, knowing the more I said the less my words would mean.

"Thank you for everything, Brother Samuel. I promise I will come say goodbye if I am able. Please rest now you are safe." I whispered the last words, hoping he wouldn't foolishly choose to fast or undergo another grueling meditation.

Brother Samuel nodded, his smile failing. "I plan to rest for a good long while, little sister. Go with the light. Remember it will always rise to greet you, no matter how dark the night may be." With that he turned to leave, his feet barely touching the ground as the other monks half-steadied him, half-carried him through the streets.

"I'm sorry you are saddled with me," I said to Brother Cristofer, not daring to look at him as Brother Samuel disappeared around the corner. "You're tired and I would imagine you wish to be with your brothers right now. I am sorry to be a burden."

"Little sister," Brother Cristofer said, his voice weary and gentle. "Look at me." He commanded. I obeyed, feeling the sting of exhausted tears threatening to fall. "You are nobody's burden." His eyes met mine with a kindness that tore at me. "It is an honor and a privilege to help those who have been entrusted to our care. The goddess chose you. I would be in direct conflict with her if I did not help."

"Why would she choose me?" I said, wiping away a stray tear. "I don't know her; I'd never heard of her before I met you."

Brother Cristofer shrugged and closed his eyes. "There is no way to know why the goddess chooses as she does. All we can do is accept her generosity and move forward." He opened his eyes and smiled. "Come, we must go to the temple to see the High One before the sun sets and the gate closes." He nodded back toward the city gate.

We moved through the streets without trouble. The solid clay streets beneath my feet were a welcome change from the constant sand I'd waded through in the desert.

It didn't take long to reach the temple. It stood on the opposite side of Sun City, a single tower rising higher than all the rest from its courtyard.

Heavy wooden doors sat open, a glowing light inviting me to enter. Brother Cristofer did not hesitate, he walked through the doors and beckoned for me to follow. I obeyed.

Once inside we entered the courtyard, and I realized how similar it was to the courtyard of the church in

World's End. But instead of ivy covering the inside, intricate carvings lined the white walls from the very bottom to the very top.

The enormous tower sat in the middle of the courtyard, also bearing etchings over its surface. Four pools of water lay perfectly positioned throughout, one to the north, south, east, and west.

I tried to take it all in, to figure out what the carvings were and what they meant. But they were faded, and my eyes could not focus.

I came to a halt a few feet away from the tower door, staring in shock at what I saw.

A young woman sat beside the door, a thin white dress flowing from her shoulders. Her skin was tanned a deep brown by the sun, her hair streaked with every color I'd ever seen.

Her eyes met mine, a perfect matching violet to the flowers back in World's End. She rose from her seat, a huge smile spreading over her face.

"Welcome, little sister." She said, hands outstretched. I moved toward her, as if drawn by some unseen force. "The sun goddess welcomes you to this, her humble home. Come," her hands grasped my own, strong, gentle, and warm. "We have much to discuss. But first, you must rest, and so must Brother Cristofer."

To my surprise, she reached out a hand to him and he took it. Sinking to his knees before her, he touched his forehead to the tips of her fingers as he bowed his head.

"Rise, dear brother." She said, still smiling. Her voice was soft, musical, and mesmerizing.

Brother Cristofer rose to his feet, tears wet on his cheeks. "I leave our little sister in your hands, oh High One." He said, bowing over the woman's hand, his lips brushing the top of it in reverence. "I will return in the morning to serve in whatever way the goddess desires." With a quick smile to me, Brother Cristofer turned to leave, not even bothering to wipe his eyes.

"You have questions," she said, reaching once again with her free hand to take both of mine and squeeze them gently. "Come, I will take you to your room and I will tell you what you must know, as well as what you want to know." A look of amusement overtook her face, a small dimple becoming visible on her right cheek.

She dropped my hands, flung open the door to the tower behind her, and gestured for me to enter.

I ventured a quick glance at Brother Cristofer's retreating figure, took a deep breath, and entered the tower. The door shut and locked behind us as she followed me inside.

Sixteen

My stomach sank as soon as I entered the tower. *Stairs.* I thought, exhaustion overwhelming my senses. The urge to fall to my knees in despair rose inside of me at the sight of the swirling staircase.

So many stairs. I can't climb them. I have nothing left to give. I looked at my companion, a sense of dread replacing every other emotion.

"Never fear, little sister." She said, smiling as she spoke. She held out her hand, inviting me to take it, and walked to stand in the center of the tower. "There is another way to ascend the staircase. Only the brothers must climb the stairs, and they do so with joyful hearts."

I took her hand, uncertain of what would happen. Instantly, I felt myself lifting from the ground as if pulled by some invisible force. I stared at the High One, too stunned to say anything, my grip on her hand tightening.

The staircase had no railing and was lit with torches that burned bright in the growing darkness. After a few moments of floating effortlessly up the tower's height, she pulled me toward the last few steps that led to a bright yellow door.

My feet landed on the steps, but I didn't release her hand. I stood in shock as she pushed open the yellow door with her free hand. Inside was a well-lit room with a wall of windows pointing due east.

The High One tugged on my hand gently, and I managed to move forward into the welcoming room. Pale yellow walls held an array of seashells, dried flowers, and colorful scarves.

Along the north wall ran a collection of bookshelves from floor to ceiling, overflowing with more books than I'd ever seen in my life. Along the west wall sat a bed, a small window, a wood stove, and an array of cooking utensils, food, and buckets of water.

The room was warm, cozy, and comfortable. It was a striking contrast to the last few days I'd spent in the dunes with the monks.

I turned back to the view out the east wall of windows. Rays of pink and gold shimmered over the tops of buildings and the distant dunes outside the walls of Sun City. Two oversized easy chairs with soft cushions sat with a small table between them.

Without a second thought, I released the High One's hand and strode over to one of the chairs, collapsing into the soft folds of it. The mesmerizing colors held my gaze, and I could feel my body relaxing to the point of tears. I allowed them to stream down my face, unheeded.

She sat in the empty chair beside me, silently watching the sunset without saying a word about my tears. As the sunlight faded, torches around the room grew in strength, lighting the room with a comforting glow. I wiped my eyes and turned to my companion.

"I'm sorry," I said, not bothering to smile and not moving from my seat.

"You have every right to tears, little sister," she replied, her violet eyes shining with what I realized were sympathetic tears. "Would you like some food?" she asked, not missing a beat. I nodded and soon a bowl of stew was in my lap topped with soft, buttered rolls.

Beside me, on the table, she sat down the largest mug I'd ever seen. Reaching for it, I realized how thirsty I was. Cold cider met my chapped lips, and I drank half of it before I was satisfied enough to put it back down. I wiped my mouth with the back of my hand and devoured the stew and rolls.

By the time I set my bowl aside, my stomach was full, and I felt warm enough to take off my cloak. I let the garment fall over the chair beneath me.

Looking down at my hands, I realized how dirty I was from the trip and wondered what my hair must look like.

Outside, the clear sky showed distant stars and a rising moons – not quite full.

"You must rest, little sister." The High One said as I stared out at the moons, my head supported by the chair.

"I need answers first," I said, my body weary and longing for sleep while my mind raced with questions. "Who are you?" I couldn't resist asking. "What is this place? Why does she want to help me? And please," I begged, closing my eyes. "Please tell me you know where my brothers are."

"I am the High One, chosen daughter of the sun goddess to be her mouthpiece to her people." She said, her voice gentle and relaxed. "I was once an orphan, left by a band of thieves to die in the dunes. My name was once Hannah."

I opened my eyes to look at her, shocked by how willingly she gave me this information.

She smiled. "Now I am the High One: beloved by everyone, protected at all costs, known by none." Her last words sent such a sense of loneliness into my heart I thought I might cry again.

"But this is a good life," she said, leaning over to take my hand in hers, a sad smile crossing her face. "The sun goddess has been good to me. My brothers have been kind, gentle, and safe. This is my home." She gestured with her free hand, her eyes full of love and hope. "This is the home of the goddess, her place of worship, refuge, and justice."

"It's beautiful," I said, squeezing the hand clasping mine. "But I'm sorry your home could not have been with the family that bore you," I said, still on the verge of tears. "You deserve better than a life lived alone in a tower, seen but not known."

To my surprise, the High One laughed. "Oh, little sister! Your words are kind but foolish. I'm afraid my family did not want me. They are the thieves who left me to die."

"I'm sorry," I stammered, cursing myself inwardly for my choice of words. "I didn't mean to offend. I should not have said anything."

"You gave no offense," she said, raising her hand to silence me. "You have no way of knowing, nor do you understand what it is to be hated by your parents. That is not your burden." She leaned forward again, reaching for my other hand. I gave it to her willingly, and she stared at it. "Your burden has only begun with the parents who lied, and the father who chose the way of fools." Her voice intensified.

My face flushed, but I was unsure if it was from embarrassment or anger. We sat in silence for a moment, both lost in thoughts likely related.

"You asked what the sun goddess wants with you," she said, releasing my hands and pushing herself to her feet. She walked over to the windows, staring out at the glowing moons. "Did my brothers tell you of her story?"

"Yes."

"The sun goddess understands what it is to be rejected and betrayed by men, by those who pledge their love and loyalty. She is on the side of all young women who must bear the brunt of the foolishness of men."

"My father meant well," I said, bristling unexpectedly at her words.

Why does this bother me? I wondered, knowing she was right. *I'm fighting for the right to not be married off like a piece of chattel. I'm running from a fate I consider to be worse than death. All because of the choices my foolish father made.*

"All fools mean well." She whispered, not turning around. "The goddess does not want or require anything of you. She desires your friendship, but her help is freely given." The words were more curt than I had expected.

She turned to face me, a ferocity in her violet eyes. "It's up to you if you want to accept her help." She jutted out her chin, her face void of any humor. "She will not retaliate against you if you decide to go your own way."

I'd never felt so small before, so like a young child being rebuked without words of rebuke being spoken. Words failed me, so I nodded in response. *I understand.*

"Your brothers came through Sun City as they fled World's End. How they survived the brutality of the dunes, I do not know. I imagine the sun goddess guided them safely here." She paused, her eyes growing distant as she remembered.

A twang of jealousy hit me as I realized she'd met my brothers before I knew they existed.

"The brothers cared for them, gave them the water they needed, the food they so badly required." Her voice faltered and her eyes focused back on me. "But Sun City is not a place for Ravens. They need to hunt, to be in the wild with other animals regardless of who they once were."

My stomach sank. *Did you think they would be here?* I scolded myself. *Did you really assume it would be this easy? Cross the dunes and here they are? What did the forest witch say? It will come at a great personal cost to you. Grow up, Sarilda.* I set my jaw as I scolded, gripping either arm of the chair.

"Where did they go?" I asked.

"The sun goddess gave them her blessing and protection to fly north." Her voice faltered again, and she walked slowly back to the empty chair to sit down. "I know they arrived in the mountains surrounding Moon Castle safely." She said, her hands folded in her lap. "But the goddess can only see so far. Her dominion does not extend to the snow-covered mountains of the witch queen's kingdom." A visible shiver ran up the High One's spine.

"Do you know," I said, trying to find the courage to speak the words. "That is, are they still alive?"

"I believe so."

I turned away, unable to bear her gaze any longer. "How do I reach the mountains?"

"The day after tomorrow a group of mercenaries will depart from Sun City. The sun goddess and the witch queen are not allies, but they are at peace. The goddess is sending back a group of traitors to the queen. I have arranged for you to accompany them if you wish to go." She stopped, waiting for me to answer.

Staring at the moons as they rose in the sky, I considered my options.

Options? Do you have more than one? You either go with the mercenaries or you go alone – and you don't know how to get to the north. You don't have any idea how to find Moon Castle, and even if you did, who would you ask for help once you arrive?

"Yes," I said. "I'll go with them. Thank you for arranging this for me. You don't know me." I turned to look at her again, offering a weak smile.

"It is a pleasure and a duty to do the will of the sun goddess." She said, leaning forward to rest her elbows on her knees. "I carry out her will with joy and obedience. But I did not do this for her."

I looked at her in confusion. "What do you mean?"

"If I had the chance of finding long-lost brothers – flesh and blood brothers – I would go in a heartbeat to find them. I have no such chance." She whispered. "You do. No matter how good and kind she may be, I did this for you, not for the sun goddess."

I reached out a hand, unsure of how to answer, but longing to bring her comfort as well as express my thanks.

She took my hand in her own and squeezed it, understanding there were no words sufficient to respond.

We didn't say much to each other the rest of the evening. Soon, sleep overtook me. I stretched out on the floor, a thick rug beneath my body, and a heavy blanket on top of me. Warmth and a deep sense of security washed over me as I listened to the High One's soft breathing from her bed.

I will find you. I told my brothers. *No matter how long it takes or how far I have to search, I will find you. Even if it's not in time to save the kingdom.* The honesty of my thoughts surprised me, but I felt no shame or regret as I drifted off.

Seventeen

The next day dawned as bright as ever. I woke to sunlight streaming through the wall of windows.

The High One stood in the sun, her arms outstretched, eyes closed, and face tilted up. A soft melody met my ears as I listened, her voice gentle and soothing. I'd never heard the language she chanted.

Pushing myself up, I rubbed my face and went about tidying my sleep spot. Much like the monks, she continued in her rituals as I quietly gathered my things together, folded up the blanket I'd slept under, and found some food to eat. My body felt more relaxed than it had felt since I'd left home. The wounds on my back no longer ached.

When the High One finished, she turned to greet me with a smile. Soon, we were descending the same way we'd risen, all while I held my breath and gripped her hand for dear life.

I left my pack but brought along my knives and sword. To my relief, she said nothing about the weapons strapped to my body. *I'm not going out on these streets without them.*

I exhaled in relief when my feet hit the floor at the bottom of the tower. The High One laughed and led me outside. The heat of the sun hit me like a wall as I squinted and held up my free hand to shade my eyes before pulling up my hood.

"How do you bear it?" I asked, already sweating beneath my clothes. "How does it feel like a weight pulling me down when the heat comes from above?"

In response, the High One turned her face toward the sun and smiled. "I bear it because I am at peace with the goddess, and she is at peace with me. We are one." I nodded, unsure I understood anything.

We exited the courtyard, walking through the quiet streets at a quick pace. We wound our way through the city, me in my hot, black cloak, her in a white dress that drifted around her like water flowing in a bubbling stream.

Every monk we passed paused to bow in her direction as they whispered a prayer to the goddess. Some she offered a quick smile, others a touch on the shoulder or a kind word.

Eventually, we came to a stop in front of a large green door. The High One knocked, and I glanced up at the sign hanging above us.

The Sun Inn. I read, the words carved beneath a stunning scene of a sun. *Kind of on the nose, but I don't expect much imagination around here.* I thought, unable to avoid the judgment seeping into my thoughts.

Everywhere I looked held a sense of sameness. The monks, the buildings, the clothing – all but the High One seemed to match and live in harmony with each other.

The green door creaked open and a long, sallow face poked out in response. The man sneered as he caught sight of us, his dark eyes shaded by his long hair.

"Come in, then." He said, pulling the door open and stepping back for us to enter.

The High One entered without hesitance. With a hand on my sword, I stepped over the threshold, meeting the man's gaze as I did. His sneer deepened as he gave me a swift glance from head to foot and waved a hand in the direction of the High One.

"Follow her." He said, pushing past me to shut the door.

Inside was cool and damp, surprising in such a hot land. I pulled off my hood and blinked, trying to adjust to the lack of light. Wavering candles winked throughout the corridor as I followed the High One deep inside the inn.

The sweat on my body turned cold as we entered a room near what I assumed was the very back of the building. The man who'd let us in hobbled behind me, breathing heavily.

"Welcome, oh High One." A deep voice greeted us, his tone sarcastic at best. The smoke of burning incense, and the scent of beer burned my eyes with its sheer potency.

The dimly candlelit room was full of large, bearded men, all lounging around tables with mugs of beer. The owner of the voice was at the far end of the room, his feet propped up on the table.

"Greetings, Oskar." The High One said, inclining her head. She appeared unbothered by the lack of respect. "Thank you for having me."

The man grinned, drained his beer, and slammed the mug on the table before him. "It's not every day the great prophetess of the sun goddess comes to visit. Would be a shame not to be blessed by your graceful and privileged excellency."

The thin-faced man hobbled over to the table and filled the empty mug with a pitcher of beer.

Oskar picked up his mug and held it out toward the High One as if to toast her existence. "Is this her?" He asked, taking a swig of beer and smacking his lips. I wasn't sure if I should be appalled or amazed by his total lack of manners.

"The girl that's meant to go with us tomorrow on our journey back to Moon Castle?" He locked eyes with me, giving me a once-over.

I stood straight, hands poised on my weapons. The High One nodded.

"She doesn't look like much." He said, setting down his half-empty mug. "But looks aren't everything." He lowered his feet and stood up. "Can you fight, girl?" he asked, strolling over to where we stood, eyes still fixed on mine.

I shrugged. "If I couldn't, what makes you think I'd tell you?" I said, body unmoving.

His green eyes lit up and he grinned. "I suppose I wouldn't. But I will require you to pull your weight on this journey." He glanced between my face and the face of the High One. "Normally we wouldn't agree to this. But given the favor the sun goddess has done the witch queen by returning the traitors so that they might face her just wrath, we're happy to cooperate."

"The sun goddess thanks you for your generosity and hospitality. Please convey our deepest thanks to the witch queen." The High One said, her voice as smooth as ever. I found myself holding back a shiver, the cold of the building seeping into my bones.

"Make sure she has something a bit warmer," Oskar said, turning back to me, smirking. "Wouldn't want you to freeze when we reach the mountains."

I nodded in response. "Noted."

The High One turned as if to leave. I turned to follow her. As soon as I did, I felt a hand grab my shoulder. Without a second thought, I twisted into Oskar, grabbing his wrist as I did so. He was easily three times my size.

Kneeing him in the groin, I shot a foot behind his feet and pushed against his wrist. He fell backward, a look of shock on his face. I pulled out my sword and placed it on his neck as he moaned on the floor. The room went silent.

"I hope that answers your question," I whispered.

He held up his hands, his face white with pain. As I pulled away from him he rolled onto his hands and feet. Letting out a slow breath, he pushed himself up to a standing position. The men around the room waited for his response in silence. I waited as well, sword still drawn, the High One standing behind me.

To my surprise, Oskar began to laugh, bending over to clasp his knees. I stood frozen in place, watching as he wheezed with apparent amusement.

"Well done, girl," he said, holding out a hand as if to congratulate me. I stared at it, skeptical, my sword still drawn. "I swear, I mean you no harm and I will not try anything. I think I'd be a fool to mess with you after a display like that anyway."

Slowly, I sheathed my sword and shook his hand, my palm disappearing in his. "My name is Sarah." I said.

He eyed me, amusement still written all over his face. "If that's what you want me to believe, I will." He said.

I flushed, annoyed at him calling my bluff. But I wasn't about to tell him the truth.

"Meet us at the gate of Sun City tomorrow at dawn." He dropped my hand and walked back toward his chair, his legs further apart than usual.

"Come, little sister." The High One said, her tone gentle. "It's time we left."

I nodded and turned to follow her, keenly aware of the eyes that followed me. Some with admiration, others with disgust. The bright sun greeted me, burning my eyes, but warming my clammy skin. I blinked and pulled my hood back up.

"That was a dangerous gamble." The High One said. I opened my mouth to protest but she held up her hand. "I do not say that as a rebuke, but merely as an observation. These men are accustomed to a specific way of life." She said, motioning for me to follow her.

"While they may serve the Witch Queen and hold her in high esteem, they do not hold the same respect for other women." She continued as we wove through empty streets toward a far corner of Sun City. "You need them to keep you alive on the way to Moon Castle. The sun goddess can only protect you so much. You must be careful."

I nodded, following along as the sweat resumed trickling down my back again. "Where are we going?" I asked, not sure what else to say.

"First, we will do as Oskar advised and find you a cloak and clothing more suitable for the journey you're about to take." She said, glancing my way. "Then we'll pay a visit to Brother Samuel. He would like to bless you before you leave. I have a feeling Brother Cristofer would be happy to say goodbye as well."

My heart warmed at the thought of seeing them again. I found myself smiling. "Thank you." I said, knowing that encompassed all I wished to say and couldn't.

"You're welcome." She replied, reaching out to squeeze my hand.

The sun rose bright and beautiful the next morning as I exited the gates and followed Oskar and his crew back into the desert. The cloak the High One had purchased for me weighed heavily in my pack.

As much as I knew I would soon need its comforting embrace, I longed to throw it off in the heat of the day.

The High One stood at the gates as I left, her dress floating in the gentle breeze, her face soaking in the bright sunlight. "Go in peace, little sister." She told me, hugging me and squeezing my hands with hers. "If ever our paths should cross again, you will be welcomed with open arms."

A single tear drifted down her cheek as she smiled at me. Within that tear, I saw expressed all the weight of loneliness from being the only woman and the high priestess of men.

"I'll come back," I said, squeezing her hands. "I swear."

"Be careful," she said, lowering her voice. "I don't believe they will harm you. Mostly because it would cause trouble between the sun goddess and the Witch Queen, but," she paused to glance toward Oskar. "They're still mercenaries."

"I will." I said, nodding my head and returning her smile. After another hug, I turned and trudged off to catch up with the group.

Eighteen

We did not rest at all. Oskar and his group kept up at a steady pace all day. The traitors they were taking back to the Witch Queen stumbled behind them, hands tied together.

There were five prisoners in total. While the mercenaries drove them forward at a relentless pace, they poured water into each of their mouths as they walked.

"The queen wants them alive," Oskar said to me, noticing I was watching as the men poured water into the mouths of the stumbling men. "I may be a mercenary, I may be a murderer, but I'm not a monster." I glanced his way, shocked by the words. "Not yet anyway." He continued, winking. He'd fallen back to check the pack animals trailing behind us.

"What did they do?" I asked, trying to focus on anything other than the endless, afternoon heat. "How did they betray Moon Castle and the Witch Queen?" I took a sip of water from my canteen. The High One had insisted on buying me one much larger than anything I'd brought with me from home.

"Much is required of the blessed citizens of Moon Castle," Oskar said, his voice quiet as we trudged through the deep sand, ever due North. "Sacrifice is among the most important requirements. Sacrificing of oneself, one's most treasured possessions and loved ones at the pleasure of the Witch Queen."

I mulled over his words, turning to look at him with confusion. "Sacrifice of loved ones?" I asked, longing for the answer to be different from what I was picturing in my mind.

He met my gaze with unwavering eyes. "It is much as you might imagine."

I shivered, even as sweat dripped down my back and soaked my armpits from the severe heat. No response came to mind.

"These men were unwilling to do as they were asked." He said, continuing his explanation after a few moments of silence. "Rather than meet their destiny, they chose to run. Now they must meet the consequence of their actions." He paused. "Or rather, their lack of action."

I continued to walk beside him in silence, horrified by what I'd just learned. I was unsure if going to see the Witch Queen was worth the risk I now felt I was taking.

"Don't worry," he said as if he knew what was racing through my mind. "She does not require fidelity and obedience of those who do not belong to her."

I shook my head. "Thank you for the assurance," I said, realizing what was bothering me. "But why do you choose to serve someone so..." The words in my mouth failed to form.

"You want to know why I would choose to serve someone with such harsh requirements," Oskar said. "Why I would willingly work for someone so cruel." His eyes bore into the side of my face.

Yes. I thought but didn't turn to meet his gaze.

"Some of us must find our own way in the world. My father was a mercenary, as was his father before him. The Witch Queen has been good to my family. I am grateful. This is my place in the world. We are not all born into luxury." He whispered.

My eyes snapped around to meet his as my heart raced. "What do you mean?" I rasped.

His eyes twinkled with amusement. "It's not every day I meet a young woman with training as precise and effective as yours, Sarah." He said my name with a laugh. "In fact, there are few young men I've met with training as good as yours."

He winced slightly as if remembering our exchange the day before. "I don't know who you are or where you came from, but I know you were born into a wealthy family. Only the wealthy have time to learn what you can do at such a young age."

I turned away and didn't answer. *What does he expect me to say?* I wondered, knowing I couldn't confirm anything else for him. We continued to walk in silence, side by side until he finally appeared to give up and moved up to the front of the line.

I did not see him again until we camped for the night. By the time we stopped, the moons had risen in the sky and the sand had begun to cool.

To my surprise, none of the spirits howled, the wind did not rush over us, and the wild dogs kept their distance. I sat beside the cackling fire eating the food offered to me, grateful but amazed.

"You can bed down here," Oskar said, squatting beside me. "I'll bed down on the other side of the fire. My men tend to keep to themselves, but just in case." He didn't elaborate and I didn't need him to.

I nodded my thanks, and he wandered off. The traitors were given food and then tied together, a guard bedding down on either side of their prone bodies. No blankets were offered.

As I bedded down beside the fire, I stared into the flames and waited for the cold to chill me to the bone. Through the flames, I caught glimpses of Oskar lying on his back, his head propped up on his bag, a knife clutched in each hand.

As my eyes grew heavy, the fire roared, and I drifted off into a dreamless sleep.

By the third day of travel, we'd left the dunes and entered a land I'd never known or imagined existed.

At first, the terrain was scattered with massive boulders interspersed with the greenest grass I'd ever seen. But the boulders soon became mountains and the greenery dusted with snow.

Freezing winds rushed down the mountains, pushing back my hood and causing me to lose my breath. At night, a light dusting of snow would cover us as we slept, the flakes hissing as they melted in the fire.

My blankets were damp all the time, constantly wet from the snow. Wearing them made me shiver but leaving them off chilled me to the bone with only my new heavy cloak to keep me warm. The howls of wild dogs changed to the howls of much larger wolves.

Oskar and the rest of the mercenaries took turns guarding our camp at night. The prisoners were given just enough extra clothing to keep them from freezing to death.

The days grew darker, but our pace never eased. Ever forward, ever upward. Ice, snow, wind – my fingers grew numb every morning, and I found myself longing for the melting heat of the sun.

By day five I wondered if we'd ever reach our destination. Food was running low, our water froze and thawed, then froze again. I was thirsty all the time, longing for a mug of hot cider and a large tumbler of cold water.

I am surrounded by water. I thought. *But somehow I am always thirsty. This is no better than the desert.* I wasn't sure how much longer I could continue the relentless pace in the ever-deepening snow.

But on the morning of the sixth day, we rounded a bend in the mountain. My eyes widened at the sight of a massive castle hewn out of black stone. The building rose above us, with no windows or lights visible, a striking contrast to the snow-covered mountains around us.

I steadied myself against a boulder, wheezing a little as cold sweat trickled down my back.

"Impressive, isn't it?" Oskar asked, startling me. I hadn't realized he was so close. Unable to speak, I merely nodded.

He grinned, pride clearly showing on his face. "I've traveled all over this world, from Glass Mountain to World's End, to Sun City. I've skirted around the castle beside the sea," he said, folding his arms in front of him. "But nothing, and I do mean nothing, comes close to the majesty of the Witch Queen's Moon Castle." He paused, still beside me. "What do you think? Is it what you were expecting to find?"

I blinked, realizing I hadn't even wondered what I would find. "It's very impressive." I managed. "Please tell me it's warmer in there than it is out here."

Oskar grinned at me, loosening his arms. Taking a step in the direction of the city, he followed in the footsteps of the rest of the group. "That depends," he said, his voice drifting back as I pushed myself forward to follow him.

"On what?" I yelled ahead.

"On who you are and what you want from the Witch Queen." Oskar shouted over his shoulder.

I shivered as the wind picked up and I quickened my pace.

Soon, we stood before the massive gate, closed to the immediate public. A guard sauntered out from the small room beside the gate, the blade of a drawn sword perched against his shoulder. He towered even taller than Oskar, his beard, eyes, and hair black as the stones of the castle, his skin pink and pale at the same time.

"Halt." The guard's voice boomed, a deep growl cutting through the whistling of the wind. "State your business with the Witch Queen."

"Don't be ridiculous, Karl," Oskar replied, smiling but clearly annoyed. "You know who we are, where we came from, and what we're here for. Now open the gate and let us in."

"State your business with the Witch Queen," Karl repeated, undeterred by Oskar's objections. "Or face a quick and mighty death."

"How about you go tell Her Majesty you're keeping the men delivering her prisoners in the freezing cold rather than letting them in to see her and face judgment." Oskar said, widening his stance and crossing his arms. His smile had faded.

Silence ensued while the two men stared at each other.

"Very well," Karl grunted. "Have it your own way." He turned and stalked back to his room beside the gate, pulling a lever as he entered the room.

The gates creaked and groaned, then slowly swung open. Oskar waved his people through, the prisoners stumbling in a line behind them. I followed, and Oskar brought up the rear.

"Who's she?" Karl barked from his room. I froze in place, wondering if I'd come all this way only to be denied entrance.

"She is none of your concern," Oskar said, his hand coming to rest on my shoulder. "Her Majesty knows all. No need for you to know all about her guests." I felt a gentle push from Oskar and my feet moved forward once more. Karl snorted, then the doors began to creak and swing shut as Oskar and I passed through them. They slammed behind us and the sound of clicking met my ears.

For better or for worse, you're here now, and there's no turning back. I thought, Oskar's hand still resting on my shoulder as he guided me through the castle. *You're going to meet the Witch Queen. You might die. You might find out where your brothers are. Either way, it's going to be an adventure.*

Nineteen

The incessant, freezing wind disappeared as we entered the depths of the castle. Oskar never let go of my shoulder.

The rest of the group dissipated, breaking off as we followed them in. Some broke off individually, others took the prisoners. Soon it was just Oskar and me walking silently through black stone corridors.

Soldiers passed us, eyeing me and greeting Oskar with a curt nod. People I assumed were servants went by with things piled in their arms and lowered eyes, their clothes neat but threadbare. Each time we passed one of them, the women stopped to curtsy, and the men stopped to bow.

"Do you always receive such attention?" I asked Oskar in a low voice.

"No." He replied, confusion in his tone. "This must be all for you."

She knows. I thought, my heart raced at the idea. *Somehow, she knows and now all the servants know too. I shouldn't have come.*

I tried not to dwell on the terrible outcomes flooding my mind. We turned into a massive corridor, the first to have windows. *We must be on the other side of the castle now.* I realized, staring in awe at the rising, white mountains outside in the fading twilight.

At the end of the corridor was an arch with two giant doors painted a deep, blood-red, sustained by black hinges as long as my arm. Two guards stood at attention before the doors. Without a word, they turned in unison and pushed the doors open for us.

The room was lined with windows from floor to ceiling, allowing the light to flood into the black space. The ceiling was hung with crystal chandeliers.

At the end of the room was a raised platform with a throne larger than any I'd ever seen. Forged of black iron, it twisted across the expanse of the platform.

In the center of the room stood a tall altar with a blue flame burning. Incense filled my nostrils, but there was no sign of the haze I commonly saw in places that used incense.

In the center of the sprawling throne sat a woman in robes as red as the doors. Her white hair fell in thick braids down to her waist.

Her skin was porcelain, her lips matched her robes, and her eyes were as black as the stone surrounding me. Her face was ageless, all at once young and old beyond imagination at the same time.

I began to tremble, half-exhausted, half-terrified. Oskar squeezed my shoulder to reassure me. We took a few steps forward and stopped again, the doors behind us slamming shut. I jumped, surprised by the unceremonious gesture.

"You are most welcome, Sarilda, Princess of Eryas." A cold sweat broke out on my forehead as the most beautiful voice I'd ever heard drifted into hearing.

Oskar's hand tightened, his fingernails digging into my shoulder. I flinched and shrugged my shoulder, trying to force him to ease up, momentarily distracted from the horror of my confirmed suspicions. He released me, his hand falling to his side.

"Please," the Witch Queen said, extending a pale hand. "Come closer."

I walked toward her like one in a trance, Oskar still at my side. When I reached the platform, I lowered my hood and bowed my head, unsure of what greeting would be proper.

"Thank you for welcoming me into your home, your majesty." I said, stumbling over the words as I wondered if they were correct. Meeting her gaze, I found her eyes boring into mine, an amused smile splayed across her mouth.

"It's not every day that I have the privilege of meeting the royalty of a neighboring kingdom." She said, sizing me up. "When the High One contacted me on behalf of the sun goddess, pleading your case, I could not turn down such an opportunity." Her gaze shifted to Oskar, the smile fading but not disappearing.

"You have done very well, Oskar." She said, nodding in approval. He bowed his head in wordless acknowledgment. "All traitors are alive and accounted for, and the princess arrived in one piece. Well done. You will be well-compensated for your service."

She shifted back to me, her smile growing again. "You must be exhausted from your journey." She said. "These mountains are unforgiving. I've ordered that your room be made up with a fire, and food laid out for your enjoyment." She studied me, wrinkling her nose slightly. "I believe it's also time you had a bath."

I blushed, embarrassed as I realized I hadn't bathed since I left home. *Two weeks.* I thought. *Two weeks without bathing of any kind. I must smell horrendous.* I resisted the urge to examine my hair with my hands.

"Thank you, Your Majesty," I said, bowing my head again. "I am deeply grateful for your generosity." My legs felt like they were about to crumble beneath me at the thought of a warm bed and a hot bath. I shifted on my feet to steady myself.

"Go now," she said, beckoning toward the door. "A maiden waits outside to take you to your chambers." She smiled and inclined her head. "We will speak again tomorrow."

I bowed my head for a final time and turned to leave. Pausing to look up at Oskar, I smiled. "Thank you." I said, knowing there was nothing more I could say. He did not respond, but a kind smile formed on his lips and he nodded.

I found my way to the doors, jumping as they opened before I arrived. Outside stood a young girl in a long black dress, hands clasped in front of her, hair piled up on her head in a white scarf. She bowed and beckoned for me to follow.

As we walked away, soldiers approached with five men in tow behind them wrapped in chains. I recognized the accused traitors from my journey, noting their change of clothing and the fresh blood staining their backs. A shiver ran down my spine as they marched passed me, their eyes trained on the floor, their legs wobbling beneath them.

The great red doors opened behind us, and I ventured a glance back. The Witch Queen stood on her platform; all hint of pleasure wiped from her face. Oskar stood beside the altar; a knife clasped in both hands.

The doors shut as quickly and unceremoniously as when I had entered her throne room. I felt sick to my stomach, thankful to be away from whatever horrors were about to ensue.

Disgusted that Oskar had anything to do with such brutality, I was also confused. *How could the Witch Queen welcome me – a stranger – so warmly while committing unspeakable acts against her own people?*

"Your Highness," the girl said, her voice soft and respectful. I realized I'd stopped walking, frozen in place. I started and turned to find her looking up at me. "This way, your Highness." She smiled, her eyes a clear, light blue.

She extended her hand. I took it, welcoming the steadying warmth of her palm in mine. We wound our way through the black hallways, some lit by torches, others lit by skylights and regal windows. I wondered at the enormity of the castle.

After climbing a never-ending staircase and traversing more hallways than I could count, we arrived at a door painted white. The girl pushed it open and gestured for me to enter as she let go of my hand.

I walked through the doorway and stared in awe. I'd expected a dark room with a small window. What I found was cream-colored walls and thin, light-blue curtains hung over floor-to-ceiling windows.

Candles flickered from silver stands strategically placed around the room. A large, four-poster bed sat against one wall with a bathtub in front of the windows. A fireplace roared opposite the bed, and a table with two chairs sat before the fireplace.

The table was, as the Witch Queen had promised, filled to overflowing with food. Roast beef with vegetables and a ceramic of soup sent steam up toward the ceiling.

Pitchers of cider and water, kettles of hot tea and coffee, rolls piled high in a basket, fresh-cut fruit, jams, butter – the food seemed endless.

I allowed the pack on my shoulders to slide to the floor as I crossed the room to collapse in the chair beside the table, not caring where it landed.

By the time the girl entered the room and closed the door behind us, locking it as she did, I was already shoving food into my mouth with one hand and pulling a mug of cider to my lips with another. Rich flavor exploded in my mouth, tears threatening to fall.

The evening went by in slow motion.

I ate until I couldn't eat anymore. The next thing I knew I was in the bath. The girl gently scrubbed my hair and combed it out in the water to get rid of all the knots while I scrubbed weeks of grime off my body.

I dug out the dirt encrusted on my fingernails and toes. The warm water felt deliciously comforting, soothing every tired muscle in my body. I was surprised by how my muscles had grown and how my ribs poked through my stomach.

The girl stood on a chair, pouring a bucket of warm water over my head and body to rinse off the remaining soap and dirt clinging to my skin. I stepped out of the bath and into a blanket warmed by the fire.

The girl pulled a chair close to the fireplace and beckoned for me to take a seat. I did so, willingly, pulling my legs up to my chest and wrapping the blanket tightly around me. She continued to comb out my hair, humming a soft tune as her nimble fingers went about their work.

I wanted to cry, but I wasn't sure what I would be crying about. A heaviness settled in my chest as I leaned on the arm of the chair listening to the tune the girl hummed beside me. Another older girl entered the room without a word, picked up the tray of food sitting on the table, and left.

"What's your name?" I asked, ashamed I hadn't asked earlier.

"Mary, your Highness." She answered, her fingers never faltering.

Having finished with the comb, Mary brought over a small table full of bottles I hadn't noticed. She stood before me, our eyes nearly level. One by one she picked up the bottles and rubbed their contents on my hair, my face, my hands, and my feet. The gentle massage made me sleepy, longing for the bed behind us.

"If you don't mind," she said, pausing and hesitating. "That is, I mean no disrespect, but would you mind if I took a look at your back?" She waited with hands folded in front of her, as though terrified of how I might respond.

I blinked, realizing I'd forgotten the scars on my back. I turned in my seat, allowing the blanket to slip off my shoulders so she could see the healed wounds.

"Do they hurt you?" She asked.

"Sometimes," I said, realizing I'd grown used to the discomfort. "But the brothers did the best they could to heal them. There hasn't been time to think about the scars."

Mary didn't respond, but I felt her gently rubbing something on my back, her fingers light as she dabbed each scar and then massaged the cream into my skin. Frankincense filled the room, pleasant and soothing to the senses.

"How old are you, Mary?" I asked, closing my eyes as I leaned on my knees.

"I'm almost thirteen, Your Highness."

I nodded in response, unsure of why I'd asked.

"All done." She said, pushing the cork on the bottle she'd just used and pulling the blanket back around my shoulders. "Would you like to get dressed and get into bed or would you prefer to sit beside the fire a little longer?"

Bed. I thought, standing in response to her question. I didn't object as Mary helped me pull on the nightgown and thick, soft socks provided for me. Nor did I protest when she helped me crawl under the covers and went around the room, snuffing out the candles.

"Will there be anything else, your Highness?" she asked softly, her hand on the doorknob.

"No thank you, Mary." I said, my eyes closing in the dim light. "Thank you. For everything."

I heard the door creak open and shut, then I gave in to the sleep my body was begging for.

Twenty

I was woken the next morning by the creaking of the door. My eyes shot open, and I sat up, reaching for my knives.

"Good morning, Your Highness." Mary said.

I blinked, hand gripping the knife as tightly as possible. "Mary?" I asked, my heart racing, "I'm sorry. I don't know, that is, I thought-" Putting down the knife, I blinked again, trying to focus in the dim daylight. "What time is it?"

"It's time for breakfast." She said, not missing a beat as she carried the tray of food to the table in front of the fireplace. "That is unless you'd prefer to skip breakfast." She turned to face me, grinning.

I let out a weak laugh and shifted my legs out from under the covers. While she tended to the dying embers in the hearth and coaxed them back into a raging fire, I reached for a thick shawl I saw lying at the foot of the bed.

Was this here last night? I wondered, reveling in the soft warmth of it as I slid my feet into slippers that fit me better than I could have hoped.

I sat in the chair and stared at the feast. Eggs, sausages, more fresh fruit, rye bread, beans, sweet rolls, and a steaming pot of tea. Mary stood from the fireplace, smiled, and turned to leave.

"I'll be back in a little while to help you dress. The Witch Queen wants to speak with you once you've had your breakfast. But there's no rush."

"Wait," I said, glancing at the empty chair beside me. "Won't you join me?"

The girl froze in her tracks and turned around slowly, cocking her head to one side as though trying to understand what I'd just asked. Her stiff smile betrayed her terror.

She shook her head. "That would be improper. Her majesty would not approve." She ducked her head in reverence as she spoke. "But I appreciate the sentiment behind your invitation. Thank you."

Before I could respond, she was closing the door. I sighed and dished out heaping portions of everything.

Way to go, Sarilda. Now you've offended the nicest person in the castle. You should've known better. Why would you think a servant in a harsh place like this would be allowed to eat with you? I grunted and took a bite.

Everything I ate was nothing short of perfect. I devoured the food and drank my fill of sweet green tea. The cold room soon warmed. As I set down my fork and leaned back, the door creaked again, and Mary entered.

How did she know I'd be done? The question flitted across my mind, but I didn't have time to dwell on it. Another girl followed behind her, took the tray without looking at me, and left.

"Your clothes have been washed and dried by the fire." She said, holding up the clothing I'd removed the night before. "And I've taken the liberty of replacing your socks. They were worn through."

I stood up, smiled, and held out my arms for the clothes. "Thank you," I said. "I appreciate you thinking of me." She hesitated a moment, then placed the clothing in my arms.

"Would you like help, your Highness?"

I shook my head. "No thank you, Mary. That is, unless you'll get into trouble for not helping me." *I must ask.*

Mary's smile went tight, but she shook her head. "My duty is to serve you in the way you see fit. I will wait for you outside your door. Whenever you're ready, meet me out there and I'll take you to Her Majesty." She dipped her head and retreated.

I pulled on my clothing and re-did the braid in my hair, checking it in the reflection of the window since there was no mirror in the room. I buckled my weapons around my hips, pulled on my thick cloak, and exited the room.

Mary looked me up and down, then took my hand without asking, and led me back through the winding halls toward the ominous red doors. Just before the guards opened the doors, Mary let go my hand.

"This is where I leave you, Your Highness." She said. I turned to face her. She gazed up at me with intense eyes. "May the Queen's mercy guide you to the thing you most desire." Her words were both cautious and reverent.

"You've been so good to me, Mary," I said, wishing I could hug her. "I hope I get to see you again someday."

She smiled again, nodded, and turned to leave. I turned and walked back to the doors, not pausing. The guards opened them just as they had the day before.

Incense hit my nostrils, but it wasn't strong enough to cover up the unmistakable scent of blood. I averted my eyes from the altar and looked toward the throne, glancing around for Oskar. He was nowhere in sight. *It's just her and me now.*

The Witch Queen sat much as she had the day before, poised and amused, her black eyes boring a hole into my head. I came to a halt in front of her and dipped my head in greeting.

"I see you've much recovered from your journey." She said, her voice like honey. "I'm pleased to see it. Mary is an excellent handmaiden."

I nodded in agreement. "Thank you for your hospitality, and for assigning Mary to tend to me. I am grateful for your generosity." My voice was strong, but emotionless.

I'd considered telling her I was indebted to her, but caution told me to refrain. *Treat this as an act of goodwill, not something to be collected in one day.*

"As I said yesterday, you are quite welcome," she said, tapping her fingers pensively on the arm of the throne. "Now, how can I help you?" She asked.

I blinked, realizing I'd expected her to offer information and solutions without asking questions. "I'm searching for my brothers," I said, stumbling over the words before my mind cleared. "The sun goddess told the High One they came here after their time in Sun City." I stopped, unsure of how to proceed.

"Tell me, Princess Sarilda," the Witch Queen interjected as I hesitated. "How long since you found out about these brothers of yours?"

"Not long." I said, my voice quiet as I tried to figure out why she was asking.

"How is it that your parents never told you about your brothers?" She stood and strolled toward the windows to the right of me. "How is it your father never went in search of them? Never tried to break the curse he put them under?"

I stiffened, knowing she didn't expect me to have the answers. "I don't know, your majesty." My voice shook, anger at my father welling up inside me. "All I know, is I must find them."

"Why?" She asked, not turning around.

"What do you mean why?" I said, unable to contain my growing exasperation. *I came here for help, not to relive or explain the decisions my parents made.* My fists balled at my sides, I waited for her to explain her question.

"Why you, princess?" she asked, turning to meet my eyes with her own. She appeared unphased by my outburst. "Why must you right the wrongs of your father? The neglect of your mother? Why not them?" She took a few steps back in my direction. "Why do you want to meet seven brothers you've never known? Why does any of it matter?"

"If I don't, then I'm doomed to marry a prince I do not love or even like."

"Are you?" She looked me up and down. "You're here, in Moon Castle, far away from your parents or King Edward and his pathetic excuse for a son." She sneered as if she knew them well. "I would be the last person in the world to force you back to a father who treats you like chattel. You would be doomed by the foolishness of that same father to live in a loveless marriage controlled by a King who cares nothing for you or your people."

"You're right," I said. "Nothing is stopping me from never returning. But as angry as I am with my father, as disappointed as I feel toward my mother, I still want to know my brothers."

I paused, considering my next words carefully. "I don't want my people to die because of choices my father made. I want them to live, to thrive. Maybe if I can find my brothers, and break the curse, we'll have a chance at another life."

"Good answer." The Witch Queen said. "Now answer me this: why should I help you?"

I stared back at her, searching her face for any hint that she was joking and finding none. "You shouldn't," I said, finally, shrugging my shoulders. "You have no obligation to help me. You barely know me. All I can do is ask: will you help me find my brothers?" I squared my shoulders, waiting for her response.

She looked away and returned to her throne, sighing as she sat down.

"The magic of these mountains is harsh. As are the laws and the people who abide by them." She rubbed her forehead with her right hand, closing her eyes and leaning back. "So am I, as the enforcer of these laws, the caretaker of these people, and the conduit of our magic."

She opened her eyes to look at me. "I know you think me cruel. Perhaps I am." Her gaze never faltered. "But I have a role to play in the world. So do you. However," she shrugged and looked away toward the windows to the left of me. "Your destiny is not yet carved in stone. Not like mine. If you continue on this journey, I cannot guarantee you'll be free to do as you please."

I nodded, finally understanding her hesitation, surprised by her apparent concern over my well-being. "Please, Your Majesty, I know what I want. I know who I want to meet and who I hope to become. You say my destiny is not carved in stone, but what kind of destiny would I have if I walked away from my people when they needed me most?"

She continued to stare out the window, studying the mountains, her jaw twitching. I allowed the silence of the room to wash over me, willing my heart to stop racing.

"It's true. Your brothers came here after they left Sun City," she said, still staring out the window. "How they arrived in one piece, none of them harmed, I have never understood. But they did. We sheltered and fed them. I tried to break the spell." She paused as if lost in memory. "However, I could not, even summoning the entirety of the magic found within these mountains."

She looked back at me, her eyes tired as she tilted her head to the right. "This was no place for them. Though they may be princes, they are also ravens. These mountains are no place for a raven, and neither is Moon Castle. They left as soon as summer hit and warmed the air."

My heart sank. *I knew they wouldn't still be here. How could they be?* "Do you have any idea where they might have gone?" I asked, tiredness creeping over me at the thought of how long I might need to look.

"I cannot tell you their exact location," she said, a slow smile forming on her lips. "But I can point you in the right direction." She clapped her hands. The doors opened and Oskar strolled into the room. "Oskar will escort you as far as Star Forest, the land of the gypsies." She said, motioning toward the man. "I know they went there, and I know the gypsies will help you."

Something akin to hope re-ignited inside my chest. "Thank you, Your Majesty," I said, meeting her gaze instead of bowing my head. "Thank you."

She smiled, this time a full, real smile. "I only ask you to promise me three things in return, princess." She paused. "Promise me you'll come back and see me someday, and we'll remain allies when you sit on the throne of Eryas."

"I can promise to return and visit," I said, hesitating and dumbfounded. "But with seven older brothers, how could I claim the throne?"

"You're right." She said, still smiling. "How could I ask something like that of you? My mistake."

"I'm sorry, I hope I didn't offend," I said, breaking out in sweat. She shook her head. "What is the third thing you would have me promise?"

"Promise me you'll find a way to defeat King Edward and his son." Her lips twitched with amusement.

I laughed. "I swear to you, I will do everything I can to defeat them."

Twenty-One

O<small>SKAR AND I DEPARTED</small> Moon Castle early the next morning. A gray haze hung over us as an impending storm threatened overhead. The wind howled in the distance.

Oskar muttered something about it being a warning sign of a harsh storm and urged me to walk faster.

I trudged through the snow, sometimes sinking to my knees and then to my waist. After a couple of hours, I wondered if I'd make it down the mountains alive. Oskar never faltered. We moved faster than we had with the prisoners, pushing steadily Southwest.

By noon we reached a river that appeared to be frozen solid from our side of the shore to the other. Oskar studied it, crouching low to the ground, his eyes drifting from side to side as I panted to catch my breath.

"What is it?" I whispered, unease filling my stomach. He held a finger to his lips and motioned for me to sink low beside him. Pulling a nearby stick out of the snow, he threw it as forcefully as he could onto the ice.

The rotting wood splintered in a million directions. Three of the largest wolves I'd ever seen sprang onto the ice from the other side of the shore, hackles raised, heads low, eyes searching. Their black fur stood in bright contrast to the ice and snow around us.

I covered my mouth with my hands in shock. Three pairs of yellow eyes glistened in the dim daylight as the wolves raised their heads to sniff the air. I realized, with relief, that the breeze blew toward us, making it impossible for them to catch our scent.

"How desperate are you to reach your brothers?" Oskar asked, his voice barely audible. "Are you desperate enough to face and fight the wolves?" His eyes never left the beasts on the ice.

"There are only three of them." He said. "I have fought off four wolves, but it came at a great, personal cost." His voice faltered as if he'd gotten lost in the memory of his statement. "What will it be, princess? Move forward and fight, or wait until they turn back and then we return to the castle?"

I wasn't sure what his preference was, whether he might be testing me.

He's never called me princess before. Although, I suppose that doesn't matter for my decision. What if I go for it and he decides I'm not worth the risk? He could easily allow me to die, then return to the castle and tell them all he tried his best.

Somewhere deep inside I knew that wasn't a fair judgment. *The Witch Queen would know, and she would not be pleased. Whatever he might think of you, he would not purposefully disobey a woman he has blindly followed for so long.*

"We go for it. I want to find my brothers." I said, allowing the words to tumble out before I could change my mind. "If I can take you, why can't I take a wolf?" I turned to grin at him. "Just promise me you'll send word to my parents if I die on that ice."

Oskar turned to me, the same smile he'd worn the day I bested him crossing his face. "Happily, Your Highness." He winked, then stood and drew his sword. "Leave your pack here. We'll come back for it."

Dropping the bag to the ground, I stood and drew my sword as well as a throwing knife. The wolves froze in place, hearing the metal scraping against the sheathes. Oskar nodded and we both leaped onto the frozen river, charging toward the wolves.

I slid but didn't lose my balance. The ice beneath my feet carried me toward the largest of the three wolves. Off to my right Oskar's sword sliced into flesh and a wolf yelped. The wolf bared his teeth and bounded toward me, paws slipping on the ice, but only in a forward direction.

He's easily three times my size. I thought, deciding on my best defense.

Pulling my arm back, I threw the knife. It lodged in his shoulder and he howled, still moving toward me. In a split second, another throwing knife was in my free hand and the wolf was almost on top of me. I sheathed my sword, grabbed another knife, and slid onto my back, dragging my knives across the wolf's belly as I slid beneath him.

Blood gushed from his stomach and he tumbled forward onto the ice, howling in pain. I whipped around on the ice and pushed myself up, struggling to gain traction.

By the time I reached him he was stumbling, his mouth snapping at me as he writhed in pain, his eyes closing and his tail tucked.

Finish him. I told myself as I leaped onto his back and reached around his neck with my knives. *It's the right thing to do. Finish him.*

One swift motion was all it took. The beast collapsed beneath me, one final howl of pain before sinking to the ice. I rolled off of his corpse and looked over toward Oskar just as he swung his sword over the neck of one wolf. The other lay beside him, as still as the one beside me.

The wolf's head rolled as Oskar's sword came down and I looked away, not caring to witness what happened next.

Silence ensued, only broken by our heavy breathing. I lay on my side, knives still clutched in my hands, adrenaline pumping through my veins.

"Come, princess," Oskar said, standing over me with his hand extended. "It's best we move out and get as far away as possible before the sun sets." I shifted to hold both knives in my left hand and took the hand he offered me. "By the time night falls, this river will be swarming with wolves. If we're anywhere close by, they will find us."

I nodded, looking down at my blood-soaked hands. I walked back to my pack, dropped the knives in a snowbank, and plunged my hands into the snow beside them. Soon they were clean and so were the knives, the only remaining evidence of my kill was the blood spattered on my sleeves.

I sheathed my knives, pulled on my pack, and looked toward Oskar for instruction. *Why is he watching me?* I wondered, meeting his gaze of curiosity.

"Tell me, princess," he said, cocking his head to the side as he pulled his pack onto his back. "What do you plan to do if you find these brothers of yours?"

"Take them home, of course," I responded, frowning. "That's my goal. I want to take them home."

"After, your Highness." He said, shaking his head. "With all due respect, you are the youngest of eight children. The only daughter. Your brothers have been living as ravens for the last sixteen years. Are you really going to step aside and let them take your father's crown?" Oskar turned and started across the river, casting furtive glances in every direction.

I stumbled along the ice beside him, thinking through my response.

"Your question carries with it the assumption that I want to be queen," I said. "That I want to rule the kingdom of Eryas."

"Yes. Don't you?"

I shook my head. "When I was younger I suppose I did. Even up until I started on this journey I assumed I would. But," I shrugged my shoulders. "I don't care about being queen anymore." A weight I didn't know I was carrying seemed to lift from my chest as I spoke.

"And why is that?"

"Because, if I were queen I'd have to go home and stay home for the rest of my life."

"It would be easier to go home, to stay there and be tended to," Oskar said, his voice lowering as we walked. We were almost across the ice. "I ask because you would make a fine queen. A royal that Her Majesty would be happy to ally with."

I shook my head as we reached the opposite side of the river and began to climb up the steep bank. "She'll have to ally with someone else," I said. "Maybe one of my brothers."

Oskar scrambled up the bank ahead of me, moving with surprising ease and speed. He extended his hand once more and pulled me up the rest of the bank. I looked up at him, realization fully setting in.

"If I became queen," I said, staring him down. "I'd never be able to leave again. Not like this. I've tasted freedom. My life was good, and I miss my home. But there's so much more to the world than I ever dreamed existed. It would kill me to give this all up." I shook my head again. "My brothers deserve some ease and happiness. It's not their fault they were cursed. They deserve to rule the kingdom. I need them. Eryas needs them."

"Then we should keep up a good pace until we reach Star Forest." Oskar said, an approving smile plastered across his face.

By the time we stopped to rest that night, the moon was high in the sky and the temperature had dropped significantly. I'd pulled out my blanket to wrap around my body as a second barrier between me and the wind.

To my surprise, we camped in a three-sided structure that blocked out the wind and left an open space for a large fire. Oskar built it up quickly from the wood stacked inside the structure. I managed to stay awake long enough to eat the food he pulled out of his bag.

"The wolves can't get us even if they figure out where we've gone," Oskar said, gesturing toward the structure enveloping us. I nodded, understanding but too tired to respond.

If the wolves came that night, I had no memory of them in the morning. I drifted off into the deepest sleep I'd ever known. Not even the dreams of my brothers crying out my name could wake me. *I'm coming.* I kept telling them. *Be patient. I'm doing my best.*

The next few days drifted by in a blur. Oskar led me through the mountains with an expertise I did not comprehend. I heard the wolves several times, but never saw them again.

"They've chosen to keep their distance," Oskar said. "Three dead and the winter winds coming in strong – they don't want to chance being weakened in number." I always agreed with him, as if I knew anything about wolves.

By day four of our journey, the mountains became hills, the snow began to melt, and the piercing wind disappeared. Tufts of grass poked through empty spots on the ground. Mud clung to my boots and clothes, weighing down my cloak. The sun shone bright above me, warm for the first time since we'd left the barren wasteland.

"How much further?" I asked, enjoying the way the sunshine kissed my skin.

"Tonight we'll reach the edge of the Marshlands. If all goes as planned, tomorrow evening we'll reach the border of Star Forest." Oskar said, pulling his hood down. I could see the sweat dripping down his forehead. "That's where I must leave you."

"At the border of Star Forest?" I asked, panic forming as I realized he'd be leaving me soon. "How am I supposed to find anyone?"

"Don't worry, your Highness." He laughed. "The Witch Queen sent word to the leader of their clan. They'll have someone waiting to escort you to safety."

We walked on in silence for a moment longer, each lost in our own thoughts.

"Thank you, Oskar," I said. "I know you were commanded to take me to The Witch Queen and then again to Star Forest. But I hope you know how truly grateful I am. I also hope to repay you one day."

He didn't answer, and I didn't expect him to.

Twenty-Two

The Marshlands were uneventful. Other than boots and clothes coated in thick mud, nothing important happened. We tramped through tall, wet reeds and sank knee deep into puddles we couldn't see.

But the further we walked, the warmer it got. I removed my cloak, exhausted by the way it pulled me down. Finding a thick walking stick to lean on, I fought my way through the mud. Bugs bit me, fog settled over us, and the hazy sun cast an eerie glow.

I walked through the muck waiting for and expecting disaster to strike at any minute. But nothing happened. The night was uneventful. Other than an owl singing in the dark as the fireflies flitted around us, we neither heard nor saw another creature that night or the following day.

As the mist faded the next evening, the ground grew dry and my feet no longer sank into it. Trees came into view up ahead and Oskar stopped.

"This is where I leave you." He said, motioning toward the treeline. I squinted, barely able to make out three figures waiting at the edge of the woods.

I looked up at him and smiled. "Thank you," I said, bowing my head. "I hope we meet again."

"As do I, your Highness." He replied, a crooked smile splayed across his lips. "I hope you find your brothers. I believe you're close. If anyone knows where they are, the people of Star Forest will know."

I nodded, my shoulders sagging. "That's what everyone has said about everyone else I've asked." To my surprise, he reached out and squeezed my shoulder, much like I would've imagined him doing to one of his men.

"Keep the faith, princess. You'll find them." With another smile and another quick squeeze, he turned and walked back into the Marshlands. I watched him until he disappeared in the mist. As soon as he disappeared from sight, I sighed and walked toward the trees.

The closer I got, the more the mist receded. Ahead of me stood one woman and two men. The woman stood a good half-foot taller than the men beside her. She wore a green, flowing dress with a brown belt around her waist.

The hem of her skirt was pulled up on the right side and tucked into her belt, revealing her leg from the knee down. A loose pair of brown leather stays were laced around her ribs and chest. A creamy lace had been stitched haphazardly to her dress.

Her light brown hair hung in loose braids down to her knees, curls escaping around her forehead, feathers and flowers woven into strands of hair. Her eyes flashed a matching green to her gown, intelligent and astute.

I glanced at the men, one old, one young, both dressed in pants the color of the sky that had been rolled up to their knees. They wore white shirts and two brown leather belts slung sideways across each shoulder.

Knives, a canteen, rope, and bottles were attached to each belt. Their dark brown hair hung to their shoulders, tucked behind their ears, and their eyes flashed blue. *Father and son?* I wondered, noting the resemblance between them.

I stopped a few feet away from them, extremely aware of how I must look and uncertain of how to greet them.

"Welcome, Princess Sarilda." The woman said, smiling and extending her hands on either side as she performed an odd curtsy. "The stars have sung many a song since I last met with a daughter of Eryas. You are most welcome." She extended a hand in my direction and I moved forward to take it, craning my neck to meet her gaze.

As our palms met, I froze in place. A surge of warmth ran through me and every memory I'd made since the day I left home came rushing to my mind. I stared at her, terrified and in awe.

"What did you do?" I asked, gasping as my hand remained firmly grasped in her own.

"Nothing that will hurt you." She replied, her eyes closed and her head tilted to one side. "As welcome as you are, all must pass the test before they enter my domain." She opened her eyes, revealing a flash of silver as she stared down into mine.

"My name is Adele, protector of Star Forest. I needed to know that what I'd been told by the Witch Queen was true." She released my hand and the silver in her eyes faded. "She has a habit of telling half-truths. But you pass the test." Her smile widened and she turned toward the trees.

"Come, it's time you had a wash, a hot meal, and changed your clothes." The men turned to follow her, neither of them uttering a word. I stood there in shock for a moment, fighting back tears and trembling as though I'd just performed an extraordinary feat.

What if I don't follow her? I considered the option. *What if I refuse?* Anger was boiling up inside me as I realized how she'd intruded on my mind, taken over without permission or apology.

Hurt pride will not find your brothers. You have no other choice. I told myself, adjusting the pack on my back. Reluctantly, I followed them into the trees before they disappeared from sight.

The journey through the forest was quick and silent. I had to walk fast to keep up with Adele and her companions. I realized how much I missed the comfortable companionship of Oskar. I'd spent weeks with him and now I didn't know if I'd ever see him again.

Keep the faith, princess. His goodbye still rang in my ears and I smiled, watching the brush beneath my feet.

After a few moments I emerged from the darkness of the trees into a brightly lit clearing. Squinting, I took in my new surroundings. The haphazard beauty of Star Forest was unlike anything I'd ever seen.

Wagons of every shape and size sat in a circle. Makeshift shacks hung with colorful blankets sat between the wagons, and strings of beads, dried flowers, and feathers hung between every shack and wagon.

Lanterns attached to poles swayed in the breeze and fires cooking large pots of food were set up beside every wagon. Stringed instruments lay propped against wagon wheels. Buckets of water sat in the bed of each wagon, and children ran between everything, laughing as they chased each other.

My chest ached as I took it all in and a lump formed in my throat. *What is this place that feels more like home than it has any right to feel?* I stopped near the circle, watching as Adele and her body guards greeted the people sitting beside each fire with a smile.

People with soft faces and bright eyes. I thought, staring at each one of them. Firelight licked at their faces, and the murmurings of animals smothered anything they said.

"Come closer, Princess Sarilda," Adele said, looking up from the woman she was speaking to. "Your body is weary and the food is fresh and free. Take a seat with us and I will tell you all you need to know." She signaled toward a wooden chair beside the fire.

The woman she'd been speaking to didn't bother to look up at me as I approached. She stirred the pot, reached for a bowl, and ladled thick stew into it. I dropped my pack onto the hardened dirt and sank into the chair, groaning inwardly as my feet relaxed.

The bowl of stew appeared before my face, topped with a chunk of bread larger than my hand and a slender wooden spoon.

I looked up to catch the gaze of the woman holding the bowl and smiled my thanks. She peered back at me, her eyes as piercing as Adele's, a hint of caution written across her face. She did not return my smile, but she nodded as she placed the bowl in my hands.

I devoured the food. The rich, herb-filled tomato broth and vegetables warmed my stomach. The meat fell apart as I chewed. The bread had been slathered in butter, soft as feathers on the inside, crisp and fresh on the outside.

I closed my eyes and ate, pretending for just a moment that no one else was there. After I'd scraped up every last drop of stew with the bread, I set down my bowl and spoon and looked around.

People sat around each fire, laughing as they ate their food. All shapes and sizes, all with the same soft faces and bright eyes. *Eyes that crinkle when they laugh and laughter that comes from deep down in their soul.* I thought, the lump in my throat returning.

"Who are you?" I asked Adele, still staring at the joyful scene in front of me, glancing between fires and wagons. "How have I never heard of you before?" I asked. "You live so close to Eryas, but I've never heard my father speak of your people." I couldn't hide the tone of bitterness that came out as I spoke about my father.

"Our people have lived in peace in this forest for many hundreds of years," Adele said, her voice soft. I didn't dare look at her. "We have survived by keeping to ourselves, by staying away from other kingdoms. We've endured by cultivating fear and respect in the hearts of men who would happily subdue us if given the chance."

My heart raced at her words, knowing she was right, but hating to admit it. "Where did you come from?" I asked, pushing forward with my questions.

A woman off to the side braided her daughter's hair and two boys ran past us screaming with laughter. A soft glow began in the periphere of my vision. I turned, my eyes wide as Adele's hands glowed with a warm yellow light.

"We are descended from the stars themselves, children of the light that guides your people when the sun retreats from view." Her fingers traced patterns in the air, creating the image of a starry night sky twinkling over the woods in which we sat.

A burst of light came as she flicked one of the stars with her fingers. "Our mother's great, great grandmother fell in love with a traveling wood carver." The star plunged toward the forest, landing in a clearing in the trees. The figure of a man emerged from the woods, offering a hand to the woman shining like the star she was.

"There was no denying love," Adele's voice continued as the pair held hands and gazed into each other's eyes. "He did not fall from the sky, but he fell for her." The glowing light faded from her hands and so did the images. "Our souls call out to the stars above us, forever connected and intertwined by destiny. Our hearts hold us here, forever drawn to this forest as the first home we've known."

I met her gaze, the lump in my throat making sense for the first time since I'd entered the clearing. Adele's eyes shone with tears. Tears a mix of joy and grief that could not be contained.

"We are not of this world," she continued, leaning forward and clasping my left hand in both of hers. "But we belong nowhere else. Until the stars call us home and the woods release us, this is our domain."

I nodded, blinking to fight back the tears in my eyes. "Why are you telling me all this?"

Adele smiled through her tears and squeezed my hand. "So that you believe me when I tell you I understand what it is to fear losing your home, to fear having everything ripped away from you."

Before I could think about it, I surged forward and embraced the woman. A deep sob released from somewhere deep inside my soul.

The hum of voices around us never stopped, as though the people were completely unbothered by my outburst. Adele held me in her arms, rocking gently and smoothing back my hair. She didn't seem to care that I was getting snot all over her.

Finally, the tears dried up and the sobs came to a halt. I pulled back and wiped my nose on the back of my right sleeve.

"I cannot change the actions of your parents or anyone else around you," Adele said, taking my left hand in hers once more. "But I can promise that we will help you find your brothers. You have traveled far to find seven loved ones you were robbed of having in your life. Your journey is almost at an end."

Hope fluttered in my chest at her words. *It's been a long time since I felt hope.* I realized.

"Tomorrow the last leg of your search will begin," her voice interrupted my thoughts. "You'll find your brothers in Glass Mountain. My son will accompany you and be your guide. These woods are treacherous and you will never find it alone."

She paused, reached out, and wiped away a stray tear. "Take heart, princess. Rest. You're almost home."

Twenty-Three

My dreams troubled me that night. Seven ravens circled me as I slept in an empty field. Every time I woke up they plunged toward me, screaming my name and pecking at my face until I bled. I would hold up my arms, trying to protect myself from their beaks, begging for them to stop. Nothing I said deterred them.

"Sarilda, why didn't you come sooner?"

"Sarilda, why did it take you so long?"

"How could you not know, sister?"

"Did you really not know?"

The questions were endless. When I opened my mouth to answer, to protest and explain – to defend myself against their accusations – their talons would cover my mouth, stifling my screams.

Nothing I thought, nothing I said, nothing I did was enough to fend them off. I half-woke to Adele singing, her hand stroking my hair away from my face.

> "Starlight singing over me
> Nothing but the light can see
> Starbright guiding every tread
> No one can change what's ahead.
>
> Starlight ever in my soul
> Shining in the darkest hole
> Starbright always kind and true
> Never forgets or leaves you."

Visions of starlight parting the clouds took over, twinkling gently above where I slept. The ravens disappeared and my body relaxed. I realized I'd been curled up in the fetal position, hands covering my face. Soon, all I saw was starlight, warmth flooding through every muscle.

I woke late, the sun peeking through a small gap in the canvas of the wagon I'd been assigned for the night. I sat up, fear washing over me at how late it was, guilt permeating my well-rested body.

Pulling my cloak on and shouldering my pack, I climbed out of the wagon, squinting in the sunshine as I searched for Adele.

Her laugh sounded on the other side of the wagon, soft chatter following the pleasant sound. *She should've woken me.* I thought, remembering the night before. As grateful as I was for whatever magic she'd performed with her song, I'd hoped to start out at dawn.

I glanced up at the sun. *It's already mid-morning.* I thought. *I've wasted so much time. She hasn't even told me where I'm supposed to go next.*

My stomach growled as the scent of food cooking over a fire met my nostrils. Annoyance flooded me, but I didn't have time to think about it.

As I rounded the wagon I came upon Adele. The two men she'd met me with and a group of giggling children all listened wide-eyed as she told a story.

"What did the wolf say when you told him you were a star?" A child asked, her face resting between her hands as she leaned forward in anticipation.

"I can't eat you then, you'll give me indigestion!" Adele responded, her face contorting as she worked a growl into her voice.

I couldn't help but smile as I thought about the wolves Oskar and I had faced and killed in our journey to Star Forest.

They don't know life outside these woods. I thought, envying their innocence. *Just like I didn't know life outside of*

Eryas. The realization stung. *Has it really only been a few weeks since I left?* A twinge of weariness crept back in.

"Now, run along to your chores, children." Adele's instructions were greeted by a groaning protest. "I'll tell you another story tonight around the campfire," she interjected, holding up her hands and tilting her head back to laugh. "The sooner you take care of your chores, the faster time will pass. Off you go!" She waved them off and the children began to scurry in every direction.

"Do you always entertain the children with stories in the morning?" I asked as she stood and turned to face me.

"Yes, I do." She smiled, warm and confident as ever. "I've found my stories help give the parents a chance to rest or enjoy a little peace and quiet. The stories also motivate quick chore work." She winked at me before her smile faded.

"Thank you," I said, ducking my head. "I don't know what you did, but I appreciate it. My dreams were cruel, and you – that is your song – took the dreams away. It's much later than I wanted to get up," I said, unable to keep the words from escaping my mouth. "But I appreciate your help last night."

Adele reached out a hand, tilting her head to one side. I took her hand without hesitation. "Just as I saw into your mind yesterday evening, I also saw into your dreams last night. It was my duty and pleasure to remove that pain from you." She squeezed my hand and released it. "As for the late hour, I find rest is one of the best ways to travel quickly." Her smile returned and she winked at me again.

"That doesn't make any sense." I said, shaking my head.

"Neither does life." She laughed and turned to the young man beside her. "This is my son, Anzel." "He will guide you to Glass Mountain, which is where you will find your brothers." Anzel's blue eyes pierced mine as he stood with his hands clasped behind his back.

He looked relaxed, yet somehow ready for a fight at a moment's notice. He'd thrown a cloak around his shoulders and a pack sat close by.

I met Anzel's stare with one of my own, searching for evidence of how he felt about his assignment. His gaze was unreadable.

"Do I really need a guide?" I asked, fully aware of how insulting I sounded, but not sure I wanted to travel with yet another man. *Especially one who looks about as old as I am.*

"Do you know the way to Glass Mountain?" Adele asked, tilting her head again.

"No," I admitted. "But surely you could give me directions or a map or something," I said, searching for any excuse I could think of. "I don't want to be a burden."

"Princess, Anzel knows these woods like I know each line of my husband's face and each star brother and sister winking down on us." She looked up at the sunlit sky, as if the stars had emerged. "He understands the treachery of the faeries, and the obstinance of the trees."

"Faeries?" I asked, nerves taking over.

"Yes," Adele nodded. "Faeries. You have not known spite until you have met with a faerie of Star Forest."

I shuddered and looked at my feet, shifting from one to the other as my back twinged with the pain of scars I had not felt in days.

"Anzel will keep you safe, he will guide you to your brothers, and he will bring you all back from Glass Mountain as well. Do you trust me?"

My head shot up instinctively at that question. "Of course." I said.

"Then, dear princess, let's get you some breakfast so the two of you can set out for Glass Mountain. Are we in agreement?"

Somewhat defeated, I nodded as my stomach growled once more.

Anzel and I walked in silence through the woods. The laughter of Star Forest faded away behind us as the noonday sun tried to pierce the thick armor of the leaves above us. The path was wide enough for both of us, but I chose to walk behind him, unable to think of anything to say or ask.

This is going to be a quiet trip. I thought. *Maybe that's not such a bad thing. Might be nice to not get close to another person I'll never see again once my brothers are free.*

The hours dragged. Anzel's pace was steady, not unforgiving or urgent. I kept up with him easily, walking in synch with his footsteps. Light breathing, the chirping of birds overhead and the crunch of leaves underfoot were the only sounds that met my ears.

The day was warm, but not hot. I was comfortable in my clothes for the first time in weeks. My feet did not freeze, my face did not burn. Muscles in my body relaxed as I walked.

"How long will it take us to get to Glass Mountain?" I asked, the sound of my low voice hushing the singing birds.

"A couple days, at least," Anzel replied, his tone gentle. "If all goes well, we should reach the base of the mountain in the evening of the day after tomorrow."

We walked on in silence. The sun had begun to set to our left, hues of pink and gold shimmering through the trees.

My stomach rumbled again and my mind shifted into thinking about what we might prepare for dinner. As if he'd heard it, Anzel slowed, glancing around the woods.

"We'll stop here for the night." He said, setting down his pack against a nearby tree. "I see no sign of faerie mischief yet. Tonight we should both be able to rest soundly. Tomorrow night we'll have to take turns." He turned and locked eyes with me, his icy blue gaze holding mine as though he were searching for something.

I tilted my chin back in defiance. "If you're wondering whether or not I'm up for the task of keeping watch, you can relax," I said, still holding my pack. "Just because I'm royalty doesn't mean I'm selfish or unwilling to do what anyone should."

His lips twitched, as though holding back a smile. "I'm glad to hear it." Was all he said before turning to gather wood for a fire.

What's wrong with me? I wondered, annoyed at my accusation. *This trip is going to feel like it will never end if I accuse him of things he's never implied.* I dropped my pack and searched the ground for dried branches to burn.

The silence of the woods became unsettling. The further I went from our packs, the more alone I felt. Every rustle of leaves from overhead or within the brush made me turn my head to search for the cause as I piled my arms high with dried branches.

"Princess." A soft voice called, drifting to me on the wind. I froze, my heart racing as I searched for the owner of the voice without moving.

"Princess." The sing-song nature of the voice, the mocking undertone, it sounded so familiar, but if asked I would've sworn I'd never heard it before. "We see you, princess." A light laugh followed the words.

A threat? An acknowledgment? What does that mean? I wondered, turning slowly and pushing the gathered wood into my left arm as I settled my right hand on a knife. *Do I answer? Or will that provoke whoever it is? Or,* I considered, *am I going mad?* The idea seemed plausible.

"Princess, we know what you want." Another light laugh followed the words, as though the creature was gaining indescribable joy from my predicament.

I couldn't figure out where it was coming from. Every time I thought I had, it disappeared and re-emerged from a different direction.

"We know what you need, princess."

I started walking back the way I'd come, hoping I hadn't gotten turned around when I wandered off the path. Rustling followed me in the trees above. I continued walking, my pace steady and purposeful.

I must get back to Anzel. I thought, relieved Adele had not allowed me to take the journey alone as I'd wanted.

Up ahead, I could just make out Anzel's shape as he bent down to stack some wood. I quickened my pace, relieved to be in earshot and eyesight.

Plunging through the trees, I arrived next to the fire out of breath and dropped my wood. He looked up at me with surprise, his expression quickly turning to concern as we locked eyes.

"What happened?" He asked, his voice quiet. He looked away and continued to build the fire. I recognized what he wanted me to do and kneeled to stack the wood I'd dropped.

"Voices," I whispered, still breathing hard. "Voices in the wind calling my name, telling me they know what I want, they see me – voices laughing as though my journey is one big joke." I choked on indignation as the rage inside me grew.

I spared a glance for Anzel. He was nodding, his brows furrowed as he glared at the wood and sparked a flame.

"Faeries." He said.

Twenty-Four

Anzel continued preparing the fire as I sat beside him, jumping at every creaking branch and rustling leaf. The sunlight disappeared soon after the fire fanned into steady flames. I forced myself out of my dread, picked up some vegetables, and peeled and cut them into a nearby pot.

"Sarilda." The voices danced across the breeze. "We still see you!" Laughter turned to hissing. I tried and failed to calm my shaking hands. "Better be careful, wouldn't want the knife to slip and cut your finger!"

"That's enough vegetables," Anzel said, his voice calm and steady. He reached for the pot and I placed it in his open hand. "Thank you." He said, smiling as he turned to place the pot over the fire. He poured in some water and a handful of beans.

"What do they want?" I asked. Unable to refrain from asking.

Anzel shrugged. "They're faeries. No one can ever know what they want unless they choose to tell you. But I would venture to guess they're bored and you're the most interesting thing to enter these trees in a long time."

"So interesting." A sing-song voice drifted down from the branch overhead. "A gypsy boy descended from the stars leading a princess to a mountain." Laughter ensued from all the branches. Anzel stirred the pot, seemingly unperturbed by the taunting voices.

"And what will we find in that mountain?" A different voice asked. "Seven stupid ravens who were once seven stupid princes!"

My cheeks flushed with anger. I wanted to fight, to scream, to burst into tears and run as far away as I could. Instead, I clutched my hands in my lap and kept my eyes trained on the fire.

"The girl who made magic sparkle and shine the day she was born is now in our forest." This voice was closer, as though it hovered over us, its tone not as jeering. "The princess whose own father sold her into slavery for a debt he owes."

The voice hissed as it came closer. "The princess who wants to help her good-for-nothing father by rescuing her long-lost brothers. Brothers she's never met. Brothers," The voice came so close its breath was hot on my ear. "Brothers who probably don't even care about her."

Unable to take it any longer, I swung with my hand, trying to catch the creature whispering into my ear. I missed and hit myself in the head instead. In return, my eyes burned as flashing light seared my eyeballs, a maniacal laugh taunting me. Gritting my teeth against the pain, I shut my eyes and covered my face with my hands.

"You think you can catch me, princess? You fool! The queen of the faeries cannot be caught by a mere mortal!"

"What do you want from me?" I screamed. "Why do you taunt me? I've never done anything to you. You don't know me." I wanted to cry, but I bit back the tears as the pain in my eyes eased and I blinked them open.

To my surprise, silence met my ears. No rustling, no laughter, not even a hissed reply. I waited with bated breath, wondering if I'd offended the faeries, scared them, or somehow created more problems.

The sound of wings fluttering in the wind passed by my left ear. I didn't move. Something settled on my shoulder. Still, I waited for a response.

Anzel bent over the fire to stir the food, pouring in more water.

"It's not often we see a traveler through these woods." The faerie queen said, her voice coming from where I assumed she'd landed on my shoulder. "Especially a human descended from a royal who does not believe we are worthy of entertaining as equals." The bitterness in her voice surprised me. "You are not at fault for what your father has done, but you are a reminder of who he is and how he chose to treat us."

I swallowed the lump in my throat and licked my dry lips. "What did he do?" I asked, not moving. *I'm not sure I want to know what he did.* I thought. *But that seems like the best question to ask.*

"When your oldest brother, Peter, was born," she began, a flutter of wings sounding as she landed on my other shoulder. "We heard the good news and sent an emissary to bring gifts and grant a gift of magic for him."

I relaxed as she spoke, her voice slowly relaxing as she told her story. "We expected to be welcomed, accepted, even thanked." She paused. A spark of light flitted before my eyes as her wings carried her away from my shoulder to a spot on the ground in front of me.

"What did my father do instead of welcoming and honoring you?" I asked, my voice quiet. Weariness set in and my joints began to ache. I squinted my eyes, trying to find where she'd landed.

Another spark of light caused me to close my eyes and turn away. When I dared open them again, a petite woman stood before me. Her skin was almost translucent, her eyes the deep green of the leaves above us.

Her white hair had been braided and twisted all over her head, drifting down her back in a cascade of lusciousness. She wore a flowing, gauze dress that matched her eyes, and in her hand she held a silver wand that twinkled.

She stood before me, her face as hard as stone, her eyes glinting in the firelight. "He tried to capture us, to hold us prisoner as common house slaves." Her voice cracked as she spoke. "He did not embrace our dignity or acknowledge our royalty. We were nothing more than an opportunity to him."

I gasped, feeling like I'd been punched in the stomach. *Why would you do something so foolish, father?* I raged at him in my head. There were no words I could think of to express my sorrow, embarrassment, or apology on behalf of my father.

"We went to your father as equals, as allies. We left as enemies. The only reason we were able to escape was because of our magic and speed. You mortals are so slow." She sneered at me, then her face softened as our eyes met. I hoped she could read in my face what echoed in my chest.

She looked away. "You have done nothing other than to have the misfortune of being born to a man who does not deserve you as his daughter." She said, staring into the fire.

Anzel was scooping food out of the pot into two bowls. He handed one to me without a word. I took it, staring at the bean and vegetable stew, watching as its steam rose in the cooling night air.

"How can I make it right?" I asked, still staring at my stew. I wondered if my question would be met with scorn, if it was too late to atone for the foolishness of my father.

"Make it right?" She asked, the laughter coming back into her voice. "You?" I looked up to meet her gaze and nodded. She smiled at me and cocked her head. "I have been a queen for almost one hundred years. In that time, many have wronged my people.

"Granted," she paused, looking me up and down. "None have wronged them as badly as your father. However, no one has ever asked how they can mend what has been broken." Hesitantly, she moved forward and leaned down until her face was only a few inches from mine.

I froze in my seat. Her features were the size of a child, but mature like that of a grown woman. A soft hand rested on my cheek and her eyes bored into my own.

"If you want to make things right," she whispered. "Find your brothers and break their spell. Then go home and force your father to apologize. Only he can right the wrongs he committed." She paused, smiling at me. "He does not deserve you, princess. And you deserve better."

I stared at her in shock, hardly daring to breathe. Suddenly, she released me, turned on her heel, and moved away.

"If your father refuses to make things right," she went on. "To apologize, then I will send a new emissary to greet him. One of war." She pushed her wand into the fire, watching as the flames licked at it.

"But, why?" I said, confusion overwhelming me. "I'm sorry, I don't mean that as though I'm questioning you." I fumbled. "It's just that, after all these years, that is-"

"You want to know, after all these years, why I am just now choosing to punish him for his actions." She said, raising an eyebrow as though my question amused her.

"Yes."

"Let's just say I'd chosen to ignore him. But now you're here. You reminded me of what happened. I want an apology from your father, or I'll enact my vengeance upon him." She shrugged her shoulders. "He'll have ten days from the day you arrive home to send word to us. If he chooses not to, then I'll come in the middle of the night. He'll never see me. Neither will his guards."

A cold sweat broke over my forehead as she pulled her wand from the fire and admired the glowing red tip.

"Don't worry," she said, without turning to look at me. "You and your brothers will be safe. I'll even spare your mother." She sneered again. "As much as I despise her for who she chose to align herself with, I doubt she had anything to do with the plot."

She turned to look at me again. "So, princess, either your father apologizes, or I," she cocked her head to one side, as though searching for the correct words. "Get him out of the way so that you and your brothers can run the kingdom of Eryas. Do we understand one another?" She asked.

I nodded and swallowed again. "C-can I ask you one question, please?"

She inclined her head.

"What's your name? You know mine, I would like to know yours."

"Why of course," she said, tilting her head back and laughing. "I am Ember, queen of the faeries." She curtsied as she spoke. "You can tell your father that Queen Ember awaits his apology."

Without another word, she flicked her wrist and disappeared in a spray of blinding light. I shut my eyes and turned my head.

"Thank you." I called after her, unsure of what I was thanking her for but feeling it was the right thing to say.

Anzel and I sat in silence for a few moments, him eating his stew, me staring at the spot where the faerie queen had just been.

"Well, that went better than I hoped." My companion said, setting down his bowl. "Now we can sleep in relative peace and safety."

I turned to stare at him. "Better than you hoped? What did you think was going to happen?"

"To be honest, I half-expected she'd turn you into a frog and I'd have to plead with her." He shrugged his shoulders.

"And you didn't think it important to tell me?" I was incredulous, gripping my bowl with both hands so I didn't throw it at him.

He shrugged his shoulders again and grinned. "I was kind of looking forward to the possibility."

If looks could have killed, Anzel would have died a thousand times over. But instead of giving him the satisfaction of the fuming words bubbling up inside me, I grabbed my spoon and ate my lukewarm stew in silence.

Twenty-Five

My dreams were a mix of faerie laughter, Queen Ember's threats against my father, and my brothers all asking why I hadn't come for them sooner. Every time I woke up, Anzel did too, staring at me from across the fire with compassion in his eyes.

The problem was, I didn't want his compassion.

The day dawned with chirping birds and rustling branches overhead. We packed up camp, ate a silent breakfast of porridge and tea, then continued through the forest.

I followed Anzel as quickly as I could, determined to maintain silence. The events of the evening before ran on repeat through my mind as I trudged along behind my guide.

As the noonday sun rose over the trees, shining more light into the dense forest, the trees began to thin around us.

The ground beneath my feet soon became rocky, boulders the size of houses appearing as if from nowhere. Flat land turned to a soft hill as I squinted through the trees. I stumbled over the uneven ground, searching for a glimpse of Glass Mountain.

"You won't be able to see it until it's right in front of you." Anzel said, turning to check on me as I stumbled over more rocks. Receiving nothing more than a glare from me, he turned back without another word.

I didn't ask for your opinion, your help, or any information. I fumed. We continued walking, the hill growing steeper with each step, the boulders becoming more frequent, and the trees and brush continuing to fade.

The afternoon wore on as the sun began to set. Pausing to glance up ahead once more, the breath caught in my lungs. The clear outline of a mountain rose before me as if from nowhere.

Shimmering hues of pink and gold met my gaze, and I realized the sun was reflecting off the stones and boulders I'd been battling against most of the day. Anzel stopped ahead of me, followed my gaze, and walked back to join me where I stood in awe.

"It's beautiful, isn't it?" He whispered.

I nodded, suddenly no longer irritated by his talking. Reaching down, I picked up a stone and turned it over in my hand. *How is it dull and gray when I look at it up close, but shining and brilliant when I see it from afar?*

"What is this place and how have I never heard of it before?" I asked Anzel, still staring at the glittering mountain before me, tilting my head back to see the very tip.

"Glass Mountain is said to be the birthplace of all magic in our world," my companion replied, his voice soft and warm. "Faeries and witches and their power – it is said that the Sun and the Moons and the Stars up above looked down on this mountain and imbued it with great power." He paused, hesitating to say something.

"What is it?" I asked, looking up from the rock in my hand. He was staring at his feet, frowning. "Tell me." I demanded.

"You should already know what this place is," he shook his head, frustration filling his eyes as he met my gaze. "Your family has been the keeper of this mountain and its secrets ever since it came into being." he gestured toward Glass Mountain, sweeping his arm out in indignation. "How could they not tell you about it? Especially when you left to find your brothers?"

I stared at him, blinking quickly as I processed what he was saying and the implications of his words.

"You mean, I could have come here first to check for my brothers instead of traveling all over the land if my parents had been honest?" The question came out as a whisper.

I didn't expect an answer. I knew the answer. *Honesty? From my parents?* I thought. *It's apparently too much to ask of them.*

Anzel studied me, compassion written all over his face. "I'm sorry." He said.

I swallowed the lump in my throat. Glancing down at the rock now clenched in my hand, I threw it as hard and as far as I could. A guttural scream came out of my mouth as the rock shattered a few feet away.

"How could they do this to me?" I screamed at Anzel. "To my brothers? Our kingdom? What kind of ruler gambles away his country?" I fell to my knees. No tears came, only a deep ache. "What kind of father curses his sons for taking too long and sells off his daughter without a second thought?"

I was staring at the rocks, welcoming the pain as they bit into my knees.

"What kind of parent never goes searching for the seven boys lost to a curse of their own making?" I whispered, digging my fingernails into my palms. "Your mother would never have made these choices." I couldn't contain the envy in my voice.

Anzel kneeled beside me, clearing his throat as he reached out tentatively for my hand. "No, she would not." He said, his hands gently unclenching my fist. "You deserved better. So did your brothers."

I nodded, a lump in my throat as we kneeled together, hand in hand, unexpected friends. As the sun set to our left, Anzel helped me to my feet and we made camp.

We passed the night in comfortable silence, each of us lost in our own thoughts as we munched on our bread and vegetable stew. I drifted off to sleep, my eyes aching from unshed tears.

I resented every step I took the next morning, my body sore and my heart heavy.

Focus on the brothers you hope to gain, not the parents you'll have to face when you return home. I kept telling myself. *Easy to say, harder to do.* I thought. *I don't know if I even want to return to the castle. Is that home? Can I ever go back there and be happy?* The idea took me by surprise.

Where else would I go? I wondered. I'd always thought of my people, people who would need me and expect me to be their next ruler. *But that changes if I can find my brothers. Everything changes. I gain my freedom in more ways than I initially thought.* The idea excited me, knowing I would have more choice in my life if I could truly free my brothers.

The mountain loomed ever closer. I didn't mind. It was a much-needed relief from the sun beating down on us. We trudged over the crystal rocks, the mountain itself growing more beautiful the closer we got.

As the afternoon wore on, we reached the base of Glass Mountain. A rod-iron door rose before us, cut deep into the grooves of the mountain face. I stared in awe, my heart pounding with anticipation and exertion.

Anzel approached the door, examining it closely as I continued to stare from a few feet away. "We need a key." He said, his voice quiet as he continued to examine the door, pushing and pulling to test if the key was absolutely necessary.

"A key?" I asked, frowning. *It will only come at great personal cost to you.* The words of the old woman in the woods came back to me as I glanced around for something, anything that could be turned used as a key. *The magic that bound them, while foolishly done, is strong.* "What can we use as a key?" I asked, tilting my head as I contemplated the problem.

Anzel didn't answer, nor did he move. I looked over at him, waiting for his opinion. He wouldn't meet my eye.

"What is it?" I asked, taking a few steps in his direction toward the door.

Anzel shifted on his feet, still refusing to meet my eye. "There's a belief among my people," he said, his voice hesitant. "That the only way to enter a magical and forbidden place is to sacrifice a piece of yourself." He finally met my gaze, his forehead wrinkled with a deep frown. "A literal piece of yourself." He clarified.

I froze, my heart thundering in my ears. *At great personal cost to you.* The words repeated themselves in my mind as Anzel continued with his explanation.

"This mountain has been upheld by ancient magic since before my people came to this world." He said. "It was and always has been a place of refuge for those who seek safety within its walls." He hesitated again, his frown deepening as he opened his mouth to speak then closed it without a word several times.

"What is it?" I asked, unable to contain my frustration. "Is there another way into the mountain?" I asked, doubting that was an option, but hoping against hope that the possibility was real.

"This is not my first time coming to Glass Mountain, but it is the first time I have seen this lock. There are many ways in, but the mountain knows what you seek. I have no doubt this is where we are supposed to enter."

He took a step toward me, his face overrun with the most apologetic look I'd ever seen. "There is no other way in to see your brothers. Any key we forge can only come at great cost to the one who wishes to enter."

I blinked, trying to come up with a way to create a key from a stone or a piece of wood. *Maybe I can make one out of one of my throwing knives.* I reasoned with myself, hating how I knew immediately that would not work.

"Are you sure my brothers are in there?" I asked, an idea beginning to formulate in my head, the thought making me queasy.

"If your brothers were not here, the door would not have appeared. We would have come to a dead-end."

We stared at each other for what felt like an eternity, the world around us silent. I broke eye contact and pulled out my sharpest knife.

"I'm going to need your help," I said, my voice faltering and stomach churning. Swallowing, I held the handle of the knife out toward him. "I need you to cut off my pinky finger." I almost choked on the words.

Anzel didn't move to take the knife from me. *Maybe he won't help.* I thought, panic starting to form in my chest.

He shook his head. "I can't be the one to cut it off." He took a step toward me, his hand reaching out to take the knife before turning the handle back toward me. "Unfortunately, you must do that yourself."

It will only come at great personal cost to you. My ears rang as I took the knife from Anzel in my right hand, nodding. My hands began to tremble. "I understand." I said, my voice faltering.

"I can't cut off your finger," Anzel said, coming closer and grasping my empty left hand in his. "But I will be right here to help you bandage up your hand when you're done." He whispered, squeezing my hand. "I'm sorry, Sarilda. This should never have been your future."

I nodded, shaking as I tried to breathe. Closing my eyes I thought of everything I'd been through since the night I found out about my brothers, my betrothal, and the way my parents had failed to act.

The protection of the boating crew, the kindness of Brother Samuel, the understanding of the High One, Oskar and the Witch Queen. My mind swam with the image of my father's face once more, my breathing slowing and becoming more even.

The same indignation and anger rose inside me, but so did something else. *Determination.* I thought. *I did not come here to give up. I didn't make it out of searing heat, freezing cold, and away from deadly wolves or nasty goblins only to give up now!*

My eyes shot open and I looked around for a flat surface. Leading Anzel by the hand, I marched toward a smooth boulder. *You must not think about it, you must just do it.* I told myself.

Releasing Anzel, I kneeled before the boulder and laid my left hand on the cool surface. Pulling all my fingers back except for my little finger, I took a deep breath and clutched the knife in my right hand.

"If a sacrifice is what it takes to free my brothers of their curse and myself of my father's foolishness, then a sacrifice is what I will give to Glass Mountain." Without another word I gritted my teeth, positioned my knife, and began to cut.

Twenty-Six

My screams bounced off the surface of the glass boulders around us, screams that seemed to come from someone else as I cut through my finger.

I was watching myself, as if from above, staring at the rock where the severed digit lay in a pool of blood. I gripped my knife was so tightly that my fingernails dug into the palm of my hand.

The screaming wouldn't stop. I watched as Anzel pried the knife out of my right hand and set it aside, his movements swift and calm. In an instant he was kneeling beside me, pushing a clean handkerchief against my wounded hand to stop the bleeding.

Darkness hovered at the edges of my eyesight as I blinked, trying to rid the center of my eyes of all the spots blocking my view.

Tears ran down my cheeks and I swayed where I knelt. In one swift movement, Anzel shifted his body behind mine and pulled me back. Still holding the handkerchief against my bleeding hand, he held me securely against his chest with his free arm.

My screams stopped. The pain ran up my arm, settling into my shoulder and sending a chill down my spine. I shivered uncontrollably, staring up at Anzel's face. His jaw clenched and his forehead furrowed, but he said nothing.

I don't know how long we sat there, me shivering in shock as Anzel bandaged up my hand.

Rocks dug into my legs, the discomfort somehow a welcome distraction from the pain in my hand. The sun began to sink below the treeline as my shivering ceased. Anzel rested my wounded hand across my chest, laying it on my opposite shoulder.

"Try not to move it and keep it higher than your heart." He said, his voice gentle and firm. "I'm going to prop you against the boulder. Darkness is coming and we need a fire."

I groaned as he pulled me toward a boulder opposite from where I'd severed my finger. Propping me up, he grabbed a blanket and pulled it over me.

"I won't be long." He said, pushing off toward the trees for some firewood. I watched him disappear before turning my attention back to the finger sitting in a pool of blood a few feet away from me.

That's my finger. I told myself, staring in a haze of shock and pride. *I did what needed to be done, what my parents could not. My brothers are on the other side of that door.* The thought comforted me, quelling the anger that still stirred inside me.

The silence dragged on until it was broken by Anzel's approaching footsteps. I tore my gaze away from the pool of blood to watch him build a fire close beside me.

"I don't know how to carve," I said, my voice hoarse from screaming. Reaching for my canteen, I held it between my legs and unscrewed the lid with my good hand, taking a few sips before continuing. "How will I create the key now that I've made the sacrifice?"

My companion blew on the fire, fanning the spark into flames. "You only needed to make the sacrifice. I can forge the key while you rest tonight." He said, his voice gentle as he perched two pots over the fire.

In the larger pot, he added dried meat, scraps of vegetables, and a handful of dried lentils to water. In the smaller pot, he added bark and leaves.

"These herbs should help with the pain," he said. "They won't make it go away," he clarified, glancing up at me from where he kneeled. "But they'll help ease the pain so you can sleep."

I nodded, my eyes smarting with grateful tears. The pain had become a subconscious roar in the background, my hand throbbing as I felt my heartbeat pulsing through the bandage.

We passed the evening in relative silence. Fatigue enveloped me as my body warmed and relaxed in the heat of the fire. I ate as much soup as I could and downed two bowls of the tea he'd prepared.

Through heavy lids, I watched as Anzel approached the discarded finger, staring down at it. His face and the slump of his shoulders displayed his weariness as he reached out to pick up the finger with a scrap of cloth torn from his shirt.

"I'm sorry," I whispered, my eyes closing. "You shouldn't have to be involved in any of this either." I couldn't open my eyes. They were too heavy and the tea had dulled the pain in my hand to a low throb that I no longer noticed so easily.

"Don't be sorry," he replied from across the fire. "Sorry is what your parents should be." He paused as if considering. "Besides, this is what friends do for each other: they help in time of need."

My dreams were blissfully silent that night. I slept long and hard, waking as the sun rose over the trees. My hand throbbed as I pushed myself up from where I'd laid on the ground beside the fire.

My eyes felt like sand as I blinked, the memories of the night before flooding back. I glanced around for Anzel, finding him curled up beside the fire with nothing more than his cloak to cover him.

Looking down at myself, I realized he'd placed both our blankets on top of me to keep the chill of the night away from me. I gritted my teeth against the renewed pain and looked around toward the boulder where the pool of blood had been. It was empty. No finger, and no blood.

I assumed Anzel had gotten rid of the blood to avoid attracting any animals that might come snooping around if they smelled it.

My companion stirred, groaning as he sat up and rubbed his eyes. "How's your hand?" He asked, staring at it as I held my hand close to my chest.

"I'll live," I said, shrugging and managing a weak smile. "Thank you. For everything." Tears threatened to fall and I blinked as my eyes stung.

Anzel smiled and reached into his shirt pocket. "Here," he said, extending his hand over the dead fire. "As soon as we have something to eat, we'll give it a try."

I stared at the tiny, pearl-colored key he held toward me. I hesitated, then reached out with my good hand and took it from him.

"How did you make it this big?" I asked, frowning in confusion at the size as I tried not to hurl at the thought of holding my own bones.

"My people are nothing if not resourceful," he replied, focusing on building up a small fire. "The trees hold many things, including sap to bind things together if you know how to use it. If you look closely you'll see the fine lines where the bones have been fused together."

I turned it over in my hand, pulling it close to my face to search for the lines he spoke of. Barely visible cracks with a sliver of yellowed, dried sap met my eyes.

"Before we venture into the mountain, we'll redo your bandage and apply some of the sap I gathered last night." He said, still tending the fire. "It should stop any remaining bleeding and will help stave off infection." He glanced up at me with a wry smile. "After all, you didn't come all this way just to die of infection."

I smiled back, clutching the key in my hand as I watched him prepare breakfast. A bowl of oats and another of green tea were soon offered to me. I tucked the key into my pocket. My stomach growled and I realized I was hungry despite my nerves.

Within minutes my food was devoured even though I only had one hand to eat it with. Anzel refilled my bowl with the leftover oats without a word. After a long sip of my tea, I devoured the second bowl of food.

The time finally came to redo my bandage and I clenched my teeth as Anzel gently undid the bloodied cloth and peeled it away from my wound. It stung and throbbed, bleeding starting up as the cloth came away.

I hissed as he dabbed the sap onto my swollen hand before wrapping it in a new, clean piece of cloth. Tearing a strip of fabric from one of the blankets, he hung it from my neck and created a sling for me to rest my hand in.

By the time the sun had reached the top of the trees, we walked toward the door. Anzel propped our packs against the mountain and nodded at me.

Taking a deep breath and exhaling slowly, I withdrew the key and stuck it in the lock. For a split second, I wondered if it would work. I tried to turn the key, but nothing budged and I stopped, afraid the key would shatter if I tried to force it.

"Please," I whispered, setting my forehead against the door and closing my eyes. "Please let me see my brothers." My voice cracked as I spoke the words, pleading inwardly for Glass Mountain to have compassion on me.

"Sarilda," Anzel said, his voice a mixture of awe and surprise. "Look."

I opened my eyes and glanced down at the key. Brilliant white light shone through the keyhole, enveloping both my key and my hand. A click and the turning of gears inside the door came to my ears.

As the light faded, I instinctively pushed on the door. The hinges creaked as the door swung open without any resistance. My breath caught in my lungs.

Anzel came to stand beside me as I stared into the cave. Shimmering glass lit the pathway before us. Hues of every color imaginable cast a rich rainbow throughout as sunlight permeated the walls of the mountain. Anzel's left hand found my right hand and squeezed it.

"You ready?" He asked, his voice barely audible.

I nodded, unable to speak, and squeezed his hand in return.

"Let's go find your brothers."

Twenty-Seven

W<small>E WOUND OUR WAY</small> through the cave, caution and awe guiding us as we walked along the path. The door behind us swung shut, a gentle click indicating it had locked in place. *Sealed inside.* I thought, torn between a feeling of comfort and another of terror. The walls glowed, illuminating our path with fragmented sunlight.

"The light can come in," I whispered aloud, trying to comprehend what I was seeing. "But we cannot see out, just like we couldn't see in from the outside."

Anzel squeezed my hand in response, looking around as we walked. I was like a child at her first ball, amazed and dazed. The path soon sloped down, widening and turning into carved steps. A trickle of water sounded down below, echoing up the staircase we'd begun to descend.

The stairs seemed unending, my legs objecting with trembling as they continued to take steps downward. I wondered how far below the mountain we'd gone. *And will we ever get back out?* I wasn't sure I wanted to ask the question aloud.

Still holding his hand, I noticed Anzel's legs trembling as well and smiled at our mutual predicament. *If one of us collapses, the other will as well.* I thought, refusing to let go of his hand.

"Who goes there?" A deep voice bounced against the walls of the staircase. We both froze. "State your name and business, stranger, before I release my dragon!"

"Dragon?" I whispered, amusement bubbling up inside me. "Can dragons be tamed and controlled?"

Anzel cocked his head to one side as his eyebrows knit together. "I don't think so," he replied. "At least, not like that. You speak and tell him your name. I have a feeling I know who it is, but it would be best if you answer."

"My name is Sarilda, Princess of Eryas." I said, nodding to Anzel. "I've come for my brothers." I waited for a response, wondering if the owner of the voice would accept my answer.

After a few seconds of silence, the sound of footsteps splashing through water and then running up the stairs was all I could hear. Anzel and I remained frozen to the spot, waiting as the footsteps grew closer.

Finally, the face of a man with a long and bushy beard attached to a body no taller than my waist appeared in the staircase before us. His legs were short and his belly was round. *I've never seen a Dwarf before.* I thought, taking in his brown pants, large leather belt, and rich red shirt. His hair stuck out from underneath a soft, green felt hat, and his feet were laced up in brown leather boots.

"Your Highness!" He yelled, glee and shock written all over his face. He clapped his hands in excitement. His eyes shone with unshed tears and he looked as though he was trying to refrain from hugging me. "You came!"

Anzel and I both winced as his shouts echoed throughout the staircase. The Dwarf clapped a hand over his mouth, his eyes widening with embarrassment.

"Forgive me, please," he said, his hand muffling the words. "Come, I have so much to show you before your brothers return." Extending his hand toward me, he waited for us to move.

I spared a glance for Anzel who reassured me with a nod and quick squeeze to my hand. Squeezing back, I let go and took another step down the stairs on wobbling legs to grab the Dwarf's hand.

"Who are you?" I asked, my hand disappearing in his large and calloused palm. Tears continued to glisten in his eyes as I came to stand on the same step as him.

"My name is Calder, Your Highness." The Dwarf ducked his head as he spoke, then returned to staring up at me as though I had risen from the grave. "I am the keeper of Glass Mountain, and of the river that runs through it." We took a few steps down, Anzel following close behind us. "Your brothers sought refuge in this mountain, and I have been their caretaker all these years."

As we descended and rounded another bend, the rushing water we'd heard finally appeared before us in the shape of a wide but shallow river. I stared in wonder at the rainbow of colors dancing across the surface of the crystal water. Fish swam by unperturbed by our presence.

My eyes drifted to the opposite shore where a table sat with a feast laid out upon it. My stomach growled at the sight of the food as my legs shook again.

"Come, Your Highness." Calder said, pulling me gently as he stepped toward the water. "You're exhausted and in need of refreshment. Your brothers will return soon, but in the meantime you should rest."

I nodded, allowing him to lead me toward the edge of the river. The cool water on my feet revived me as we splashed through. Fish started and swam in every direction to avoid us. Soon we were out of the water and Calder was leading me toward a single chair at the head of the table.

My head swam as I sat down. *What is this feeling?* I wondered, shutting my eyes to combat the way the light-filled cavern was beginning to spin. *Overwhelm? Relief? Or is it just my stupid finger?* My bandaged hand came to rest in my lap, covered by my good hand.

"What you feel is everything all at once, Your Highness." Calder's gentle voice forced open my eyes. I turned to meet his gaze, shocked at his comment. We were eye-level now, him standing beside me, studying my face as I sat slumped in the chair.

"How did you know that?" I asked, horrified by what else he might find in my mind if he could read me so easily.

"The Mountain knows all the secrets of those who venture into its heart." He held out his hand again. Reluctantly, I placed my wounded hand in his calloused palm. "No need to fear," he continued. "The Mountain will protect those secrets, and so will I." Without another word, he beckoned for me to eat while he unwrapped the bandage on my hand.

Looking away from the Dwarf, I did as I was told and piled my plate high with food. Anzel joined me, perching on the edge of the table. Calder paid us no mind as we ate. He meticulously cleaned my wound. Wandering off and returning with a salve, he bandaged it back up with clean wrappings. By the time he was done, I realized the dull throbbing had ceased.

"Thank you." I said, smiling.

The next couple of hours passed in silence. Anzel and I finished eating and stared at the cavern around us. Calder busied himself about the table, humming a low tune as he set out more food and cleaned up our mess.

The sudden whirring of wind caused me to glance up at the ceiling. I realized there was an opening in the mountain, just large enough for light to stream in and small animals to fit. *Small animals like a bird.* I realized.

"Your brothers have arrived." Calder said, pulling on my good hand to help me stand. "Come, you and your companion must watch from behind this boulder." He gestured toward a massive rock off to the side.

Surprising myself, I obeyed without questioning why we needed to hide behind a boulder. The sound of flapping wings filled the cavern as soon as we'd hidden ourselves. I peered around the corner to watch as seven ravens descended from the opening in the ceiling. They perched on top of the table, pulling their wings in against the side of their bodies. Pecking at the food laid out for them, they stopped and tilted their heads at one another.

"Someone has been here, Calder." The largest raven cried out. His voice was a strange mix of a caw and a voice that reminded me of my father. I swallowed the emotion filling my throat, determined not to cry.

"Our sister." The smallest raven cried, lifting his head to caw at the ceiling as he jumped around on the table searching for me. "Where is she, Calder? Where is our sister?" The others joined in the cry, jumping around as they searched for a glimpse of me.

Unable to hesitate any longer, I ran out from my hiding place, unsure of what would happen. In the blink of an eye the ravens transformed from seven hopping birds to seven young men falling off the table. In an instant, they were on their feet and I found myself enveloped in seven pairs of arms.

A mix of laughter and sobs filled the cavern, my brothers laughing with joy as I sobbed with relief.

"You came for us," One said, clasping my face between his hands. Eyes that resembled my mothers stared down at me. "I'm Alexander, your second oldest brother." He said, pulling me in for a hug. "That's Wolfgang, and Peter the oldest," he pointed to his left. "And that's Andreas and Johann," he pointed to his right. "And that's Friedrich and Ernst, the youngest of us all." He said, pointing behind me and turning me around to face each name.

"You came for us." Ernst said, tears threatening to fall as he reached out a hand to pull me away from Alexander. "Mother and Father didn't come for us, but you did."

His words split my heart in two and I clung to him, unable to speak as I continued to sob. For a few moments everything stilled as Ernst hugged me. No whispers, no more laughter, just the sound of my sobs echoing throughout the cavern. Ernst clung to me, smoothing back my hair as I cried. Eventually the tears ran out and I pulled away.

Suddenly embarrassed, I glanced around at the seven new pairs of eyes studying me. "I'm sorry," I said, wiping my nose with my forearm. "I didn't mean to cry like that."

"We don't even know your name," Peter said, father's voice coming out of his mouth once more.

I laughed. "My name is Sarilda." I said, continuing to wipe my face clean with my sleeve. Glancing around on tiptoe, I found Anzel leaning against the boulder we'd hidden behind. "And this is my friend, Anzel." I motioned for him to join us as my brother's eyes turned to look at him.

Anzel pushed away from the boulder and inched toward us, his face betraying his discomfort.

"You broke the curse," Wolfgang said, smiling down at me. "You found us."

I shook my head, confusion setting in. "I don't understand what I did though," I said, looking at each of them in turn before searching for Calder. "How did I break the curse?"

Calder cleared his throat and I turned to find him standing on top of the table, his head just higher than Peter's.

"You dared to care." He said, smiling. "The curse placed upon your brothers was one of carelessness. All that was required to break it was for someone who loved them to care enough to find them. No matter how difficult your journey became, you never gave up. Unlike your parents, you dared to care, even when it meant you would suffer."

I blinked, processing his words. "You mean," I said, swallowing and clearing my throat. "My parents could have broken the curse long ago if they just hadn't given up searching for them?"

Calder nodded. We all stood in silence for a few minutes, the reality of Calder's words washing over us.

"Well," Friedrich said, shrugging his shoulders as a sly smile blossomed over his face. "I haven't eaten yet, and I'm pretty sure this is going to be the best meal I've tasted in sixteen years." He grinned, his teeth flashing and his eyes gleaming with excitement. "If it's all the same to the rest of you, I'd like to eat before we leave."

In an instant, all seven brothers swarmed the table, sitting on it as they pulled heaping plates of food onto their laps. Anzel sidled up beside me and took my good hand in his.

"You did it." He said.

I nodded. "I did it."

Epilogue

The time has come to end my story, dear reader. But I do not wish to leave you in the dark about what happened once we returned home.

The journey back to the Kingdom of Eryas was uneventful at best, but also the most enjoyable few days I'd ever experienced. Anzel happily led us through the forest and back to the castle.

My brothers spent our days telling me all about their time as ravens. They spoke of challenges, triumphs, and hilarity. I spent our evenings telling them what life was like growing up without them.

Laughter followed us, and so did bickering. But my heart was full.

We arrived at the castle four days after leaving Glass Mountain, and three days before the deadline given by King Edward. We were met with stunned guards who rode out to investigate our party. When Captain Bastian saw my face, he dismounted from his horse and embraced me. Grinning at my brothers, he and his soldiers escorted us all inside the gates of the castle.

My mother met us in the courtyard, flinging her arms around me and weeping. She didn't know how to greet my brothers, and they didn't know how to greet her. I wondered for a moment if they would flee as they realized this castle was no longer their home. But, to my relief, they stayed beside me and embraced the silent awkwardness that fell over us all.

My father exited the castle doors next, his eyes wide and his face pale. Glancing between all of us, his eyes wavered as they met mine. In the blink of an eye, he kneeled before us and begged our forgiveness.

When I say I did not know how to respond to his pleas, I am not exaggerating. As angry as I'd been, as angry as I still was, I didn't know how to respond to my father begging for our forgiveness. When I looked to my brothers and Anzel, I realized they didn't know what to do either.

But soon, Peter had enough of Father's pleading and Mother's tears. "Enough," He exclaimed, exasperation all over his face. "Spare us the fine words and the heartfelt apologies."

Their silence ensued, and Peter's words gave me the boldness I'd been looking for.

"King Edward will be here in three days." I said, shaking off Mother and stepping forward as I raised my voice to be heard throughout the courtyard. "My brothers and I will deal with him when he arrives. You," I said, looking from Father to Mother and back again. "Will journey back to the forest to apologize to Queen Ember."

My eyes bore into Father's as his widened in terror and his mouth dropped open.

"No arguments." I said, holding up my hand. "I didn't travel the whole of our land to find my brothers for you to argue with me now." I nodded to Captain Bastian. "Please ask for their horses to be saddled and for two of your best men to accompany them, Captain."

The Captain bit back a smile as he nodded and turned to do as I asked.

"Now," I said, turning back to Mother and Father. "Go pack. You'll leave within the hour."

Reader, to my surprise, they did as I said. Father rose from his knees and Mother turned back to the door to pack. Within an hour, both of them mounted their horses and rode away with the soldiers provided.

King Edward arrived three days later, as expected, to a castle run by seven young princes and a princess who met him outside the gates. He eyed me from where he stood with his hand resting on his sword. His face was frozen in an uncertain grin, hostility practically oozing from his pores.

"Princess Sarilda," he said, taking a step toward me as he glanced at Captain Bastian, Peter, and Ernst standing a few feet behind me. "What a pleasure to greet you." He gave a slight bow as he took in the scenery. The gates to the castle had been closed, and soldiers stood at the ready along the walls and in the towers.

"You can skip the pleasantries, King Edward." I said, not returning his bow with a curtsy. "We know why you're here. Why you and your son have come." I said, glancing at the boy.

I was unsurprised to learn that Prince Henry was the one with rotting teeth who my mother had saved me from during my birthday celebration. He was frozen in place, his hands behind his back, and his eyes wide. A nasty sneer turned up his lip as he watched the scene unfold before him.

"Where is your father, young lady?" King Edward bit out, his grin replaced with fury. "How dare you address me in such a disrespectful manner."

"The King is not here." I said, shrugging my shoulders and holding up a hand the same way I'd done with my father. "He had business with Faerie Queen Ember and will not return for another few days." I took a step forward, my hand perched on my sword. "You can deal with me, my brothers, and Captain Bastian." I said, nodding toward the three men behind me.

"I've come to collect on the debts owed by your father." He said, straightening his back and glaring down at me. "Gather your things and meet us back here within an hour, or else-"

"Or else what?" I interrupted again, stepping close enough that we could shake hands. "You'll kill me where I stand? You'll destroy Eryas?" I met his gaze with my own bubbling wrath. "Your debt is not with me, nor is it with my brothers or the rest of the Kingdom of Eryas. Your debt is with my father. He is not here, and we will not pay what he owes you."

I took one more step, my eyes never leaving his as I spoke in a hushed tone. "I, specifically, will not allow you to take me the way you might take a horse to repay a gambling debt." I nodded toward the prince. "Go find your son a bride somewhere else. Get out of my kingdom and never come back."

King Edward stared at me in shock, fury flashing over his face as he considered my words. His face turned purple with rage.

"Why you-" He screamed, reaching out a hand as if to grab me, but in an instant he was on his back with my foot pressed against his windpipe.

"Take one more step in my direction and I swear on the two moons that I will end him." I said, not bothering to look up at the prince and the soldiers who had taken some startled steps forward as they'd drawn their swords. King Edward sputtered beneath my foot, staring up at me with hatred and surprise.

"I'll give you one final chance," I said, bending over him. "Leave Eryas, and never come back. My father's debt to you is forgiven. Anything you did for him is nothing more than a sign of good faith between kingdoms now." I waited for the king to answer, not releasing my foot until he nodded and choked out his agreement.

Allowing him to stand, I backed away and brushed myself off. "Safe journey home, your majesty." I said with a slight bow of the head.

Within an hour, we had confirmation that King Edward, Prince Henry, and their entire ship of soldiers had left the harbor. As hoped, they never returned.

The celebration feast we indulged in that evening was unlike any I'd ever enjoyed. We laughed, we sang, we danced – everyone in the castle was made to enjoy themselves late into the night. The next morning Mother and Father returned, their faces weary and their dispositions humbled.

Though my father still wore the crown, Peter took over as the authority all obeyed. He reigned as a kind prince, and a generous sovereign, even marrying a woman from a neighboring kingdom.

The rest of my brothers fell into routine where they were needed. Alexander and Wolfgang bolstered Captain Bastian's training, growing the army both in number and in skill. Andreas and Johann oversaw the cultivation of our fields, using knowledge they'd learned from their time as ravens to help our farmers grow larger and stronger crops. Friedrich took over the pitiful fleet of ships we had. Working with Captain Bastian, he created a defense to be reckoned with by those who might attack us by sea.

And Ernst? He and I took advantage of our natural birth order. Having spent most of his life traveling the land, he itched and ached to travel again. So did I. With the blessings of our older brothers, the reluctance of our parents, and the company of Anzel, we became the first ambassadors of Eryas.

Even now, as I sit beside the fire and glance up at the sea of stars above me, my mind still spins as I write my story. Anzel and Ernst are the best friends I could ever ask for. Their loyalty and love fill my heart as I strive to return their friendship. We return frequently to Star Forest, The Sun, and Moon Castle before traveling home to Eryas. But we never remain still for longer than a week or two.

Our hearts are set on the adventure we find along the paths we travel.

The End

MANY THANKS

To my husband, Brian: this book would not exist without you. Thank you for never giving up on me and never allowing me to give up either. No one else knows how much of myself is poured into the stories I write or how much they mean to me. No one else witnesses the bad days, the crazy times, the obsessive hours, or the distracted looks. You're the only one who sees just how much my writing takes out of me while simultaneously bringing me life. I love you forever.

To my author twin, Ellen Vandever: thanks for always telling me to keep going and never give up.

To my Beta readers: Samantha, Lisa, Sarah, and Gracia – thank you for all you do.

To my sister and chapter artist, Corrie: You took the most vague brief and created something breathtaking.

Thank you for making my book come alive in wonderful, beautiful ways.

To my Mommy: thanks for loving me and keeping me going on hard days. Thank you for reading everything I write and recommending it to everyone you know.

To my Mother-in-law: you're the best bonus mom a girl could ask for. Thanks for always reading my work and encouraging me to keep going.

To my Aunt Kathy and my Aunt Trish: you both are my heroes. I love you.

ABOUT THE AUTHOR

 As a child, Ellen dreamed of writing books, acting in plays, and going on adventures. She read books, played in the dirt, and sewed herself costumes as she got older. Adulthood took over for a while and creativity took a backseat. One day she recognized the longing to write again and picked up an old story. 18 months later *Child of Shadows* was born.

Ellen currently lives a quiet life in North Carolina with her husband, Brian. In her spare time, she enjoys sewing, spending time with friends, and watching TV.

Her current dreams include renovating an old house, making a full-time living with her writing, and learning to garden.

To watch her journey, access full color maps, character name lists, and learn more about her, check out her online presence below.

www.authorellenceely.com
Instagram: @authorellenesceely
TikTok: @author_ellenesceely

Also By

"I got tired of letting the darkness win."

In the gritty depths of the Slums of Shantu, where poverty and crime reign unchecked, lies a tale of resilience, magic, and untold power. Eliora, a spirited orphan, finds herself on a perilous journey in the haunted land of Zale as she seeks to defeat an evil witch hungry for absolute control.

On a quest for the mystical book that wields dominion over nightmares, Eliora's fate becomes intertwined with that of Hadithi, a mysterious figure known only as a Shadow of Shantu.

As Eliora navigates the treacherous landscape of Zale, she learns that her abilities far surpass her humble beginning. Alongside a determined warrior seeking redemption for his father's crimes, Eliora must confront her deepest fears and harness her newfound strength to confront the darkness threatening to engulf the world.

In a world where nightmares come to life, Eliora's journey is only just beginning, and the true extent of her power is yet to be revealed.

Buy on Amazon: https://a.co/d/5hSBKji

The people of the Slums were left to rot. Governor Aepep sat in his mansion. Starving children wandered the Slums of Shantu.

Yuvraj and Tyr dream of the day when they might take their rightful place as children of the governor who disowned them. Together they choose to fight the tyranny, training with an Elf named Chantrea. Gathering other orphaned children like themselves, the two boys organize a rebellion as they aid the people of the Slums.

Will this fight become a drop of hope in a sea of misery or burn on the battlefield before it's truly begun?

Into the shadows you cast us,
So, from the shadows we rise,
Until, as Shadows, we emerge:
victorious.
We're coming.

Son of Kings is a Prequel to *Child of Shadows* and Book Two in the series *The Legends of Zale*. Told by Yuvraj, it reveals the origins of the Shadows of Shantu and centers around the conflict swirling inside Yuvraj as he seeks to find his place in the world.

Buy on Amazon: https://a.co/d/7bmr6CU

Made in the USA
Middletown, DE
25 March 2025